TO ENTANGLE A HEART

THE FOUR KINGDOMS AND BEYOND

THE FOUR KINGDOMS

The Princess Companion: A Retelling of The Princess and the Pea (Book One)

The Princess Fugitive: A Reimagining of Little Red Riding Hood (Book Two)

The Coronation Ball: A Four Kingdoms Cinderella Novelette

Happily Every Afters: A Reimagining of Snow White and Rose Red (Novella)

The Princess Pact: A Twist on Rumpelstiltskin (Book Three)

A Midwinter's Wedding: A Retelling of The Frog Prince (Novella)

The Princess Game: A Reimagining of Sleeping Beauty (Book Four)

The Princess Search: A Retelling of The Ugly Duckling (Book Five)

BEYOND THE FOUR KINGDOMS

A Dance of Silver and Shadow: A Retelling of The Twelve Dancing Princesses (Book One)

A Tale of Beauty and Beast: A Retelling of Beauty and the Beast (Book Two)

A Crown of Snow and Ice: A Retelling of The Snow Queen (Book Three)

A Dream of Ebony and White: A Retelling of Snow White (Book Four)

A Captive of Wing and Feather: A Retelling of Swan Lake (Book Five)

A Princess of Wind and Wave: A Retelling of The Little Mermaid (Book Six)

RETURN TO THE FOUR KINGDOMS

The Secret Princess: A Retelling of The Goose Girl (Book One)

The Mystery Princess: A Retelling of Cinderella (Book Two)

The Desert Princess: A Retelling of Aladdin (Book Three)

The Golden Princess: A Retelling of Ali Baba and the Forty Thieves (Book Four)

The Rogue Princess: A Retelling of Puss in Boots (Book Five)

The Abandoned Princess: A Retelling of Rapunzel (Book Six)

FOUR KINGDOMS DUOLOGY

To Ride the Wind: A Retelling of East of the Sun and West of the Moon (Book One)

To Steal the Sun: A Retelling of East of the Sun and West of the Moon (Book Two)

FOUR KINGDOMS FAIRY TALE NOVELLAS

To Ensnare a Prince: An Entwined Prince and the Pauper Retelling (Book One)

To Entangle a Heart: An Entwined Prince and the Pauper Retelling (Book Two)

TO ENTANGLE A HEART

AN ENTWINED PRINCE AND THE PAUPER RETELLING

FOUR KINGDOMS FAIRY TALE NOVELLAS BOOK 2

MELANIE CELLIER

LUMINANT PUBLICATIONS

*After ten years, this one is once again for Marc—
the one who entangled my heart*

Four Kingdoms
Northhelm
NORTHGATE
Rangmeros
Rangmere
Arcadia
Kuralan
ARCADIE
The Great Desert
KAREMA
LANARE
Lanover
SIRKALA
Ardasira
INVERNE
BANISHMENT ISLAND

PROLOGUE

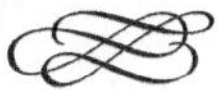

LEO

Crown Prince Leo of Lanover stared down at the papers on the desk in front of him with unseeing eyes. Even when the study door opened, he didn't look up.

"What's this?" asked a voice as familiar as his own. "I thought you were eager to see the tour off—finally being entrusted with a responsible role and all that. If you're having second thoughts, it's a bit late now. The real adults won't be back for weeks. You're stuck with just me."

Leo looked up at his cousin, now perched on the other side of the desk, one leg swinging. Luca had been born only three months after Leo and had always been more like a twin to him than a mere cousin.

"I *was* excited about it," he said, "until my parents made a last minute confession."

"That sounds ominous." Laughter edged Luca's voice, but Leo only grimaced.

"Turns out I have an extra responsibility to fulfill—one they forgot to warn me about ahead of time."

Luca grinned. "Considering Uncle Frederic's excellent

memory, I assume it must be dire. Don't tell me they've left the Dowager Duchess to nursemaid us, after all."

"Worse," Leo said grimly.

Luca's eyebrows rose. "Worse? Don't spare my feelings —tell me immediately!"

"It isn't an elderly lady we're being saddled with but a young one. A beautiful one our own age."

Luca's eyes narrowed. "That doesn't sound dire to me." He grinned. "Quite the opposite, in fact."

"For you, perhaps, but not for me. My parents have *hopes*."

"Hopes?" Luca straightened, slipping off the edge of the desk. "You can't be serious! Who is she?"

"Princess Rose of Arcadia. King Max and Queen Alyssa's only daughter."

Luca whistled. "They're serious, then! The Dowager Duchess has been pushing for a closer alliance with Arcadia forever." He frowned. "But what about the High King and all his decrees about kingdoms being ruled by love? Uncle and Father were both allowed to choose their own brides. I thought for sure they'd want a love match for you at least."

"That's the worst of it," Leo said with a groan. "I haven't just been *encouraged* to make an advantageous marriage, I've been ordered to fall in love first."

Luca laughed. "As easy as that, is it?"

Leo glared at him. "You can laugh! No one is cold-bloodedly arranging your 'love match' ahead of time."

"If she's sufficiently beautiful and charming, I might be amenable," Luca said with a grin. "But my parents don't consider me sober enough for marriage yet." His eyes twinkled as he looked at his cousin. "They're hoping your newfound responsibility will rub off on me. I heard the twins talking about it."

Leo laughed in spite of himself. Luca's younger sisters had always been a useful source of information to the older boys. They could never resist discussing every interesting tidbit they picked up.

"So do you mean to oblige your parents?" Luca watched his cousin with a gleam of genuine curiosity in his eyes.

Leo squared his shoulders. "Of course not."

When his grandparents retired and his parents ascended to the throne, everything had changed. They weren't just his parents anymore, but King Frederic and Queen Evangeline. And that made him crown prince. He had intended to work hard during their absence and prove to them that he was ready to take on the responsibility of his new role. But while Leo was ready to dedicate his life to Lanover, he wanted a wife of his own choosing to partner with him in that effort.

It was outrageous of his parents—who had always championed the High King's ways—to suddenly talk of marriage alliances. Even if Princess Rose had been raised as royalty and therefore *understood the burdens and responsibilities of the role.* His eyes narrowed as he thought of his father's earnest words.

He knew his parents genuinely thought the Arcadian princess would be a good match for him. But his mother had married his father without any royal experience, and she had excelled in her role as crown princess. Leo was certain any bride he chose would do the same.

He ran a hand down his face. "I had so many plans for

these weeks—projects I wanted to take on." He sighed. "And now I'll be spending my time dancing attendance on a princess who's probably expecting a proposal at the end of her visit."

"We could always switch places," Luca said. "Or are you too responsible for tricks these days?"

Leo's head snapped up at the slight mockery in Luca's tone, but the teasing expression on his cousin's face took any sting from his words. Leo laughed. Thank goodness Luca hadn't gone on the tour. He always knew how to lighten Leo's dark moods.

Leo stood and stretched. "Princess Rose might not know the two of us apart, but our own court certainly does —not to mention every servant and official at the palace."

Luca laughed, clearly having achieved his purpose with the suggestion.

"Do you ever miss those days?" he asked, a little wistfully.

Leo didn't respond because he didn't know what to say. Some days he missed his old carefree life, but other days he relished the chance to be involved in things that really mattered. He wasn't a child anymore.

He squared his shoulders. But that didn't mean he had to fall in love with a stranger on command. He might be ready for more responsibility, but the old him hadn't entirely disappeared either. He couldn't stomach being bound for the rest of his life to a girl who hadn't even chosen him for herself.

An idea occurred to him, and he turned to Luca with a glimmer of his old mischief.

"Actually, switching places isn't a terrible idea."

Luca looked alarmed. "Thousands of people trying to keep a secret, remember? I was only trying to make you laugh."

Leo shook his head. "Obviously we can't swap identities, but that doesn't mean you can't take on my role. Unofficially, of course."

Luca frowned. "I have no dreams of playing crown prince—even temporarily."

"I'm more than willing to do the crown prince duties—it's the entertaining a princess part I'm not keen on. But we can't abandon a visiting royal entirely either. Someone will have to entertain her—but it doesn't have to be me. There's a second Lanoverian prince on hand, after all." He gave Luca a wicked grin. "And don't try to claim you don't want to—you already said you liked the idea of spending time with a beautiful young lady."

Luca laughed and held up his hands in surrender. "I walked straight into that one, didn't I? Loaded the bow for you and everything."

"So you'll do it?" Leo asked quickly.

Luca clapped him on the shoulder. "Of course I'll do it." He smirked. "I'll even do my best to enjoy the ordeal." Leo grinned broadly, but Luca's voice turned stern. "As long as you don't get any ideas about redirecting your parents in my direction. I have no more interest in marriage alliances than you do."

Leo's grin didn't falter as weight lifted from his shoulders. "There's no need to worry about that. King Max and Queen Alyssa dote on their daughter. They won't consider sending her away from Arcadia unless it involves stepping up from princess to future queen." He shook his head.

"Apparently they're just as convinced as my parents that she'll make an excellent queen."

"That's all right, then," Luca said, his cheerfulness restored. "You focus on managing the palace in your parents' absence and leave the job of charming foreign princesses to me. It's just playing to our strengths, really."

With which parting shot he whisked himself back out of the room before Leo could protest.

CHAPTER 1

𝒫rincess Rose looked across the carriage at her odd traveling companion, discontent swelling inside her. Natalie buzzed with an underlying excitement about their journey that Rose couldn't muster. And it wasn't the only difference between them. Everything about Natalie seemed opposite to Rose's carefully controlled existence.

Not that Rose's feelings were in any way Natalie's fault. Natalie was only a new acquaintance, and Rose's discontent had been brewing for a long time. She should keep quiet as she usually did and not burden Natalie with her chaotic emotions.

Words burst out of her. "When my brother turned eighteen, he went traveling alone and got into all sorts of trouble. We didn't even know if he was alive! But I've always been a dutiful, obedient, perfect princess."

Natalie's eyes widened at the unexpected explosion of words. "Is that…a problem?"

"Even I have my limits!" Rose exclaimed, abandoning

the last of her usual caution—a caution honed by nineteen years of royal life. "I'm not obediently trotting off to Lanover to marry Crown Prince Leo like everyone wants!"

She waited breathlessly for Natalie's disapproval—or at least, surprise. Everyone knew how valuable it would be for Arcadia to have closer ties with their wealthy ally, Lanover. And everyone thought it was perfect that Princess Rose of Arcadia and Crown Prince Leo of Lanover had been born only two months apart.

She had heard the whispers all year. *Like they were meant to be.*

Even Rose's parents had hinted at their hopes for an alliance—although of course they would never force her into the marriage against her wishes. They knew all too well that the High King blessed those kingdoms ruled by love.

But that didn't stop them hoping—and their hope hurt worse than harsh commands would have done. An order could have been rejected in a spirit of righteous indignation. But Rose's parents loved her, and she loved them. She had spent her whole life following their example and doing her best to be the ideal princess that Arcadia deserved. She had never once wanted to make them worry—and she still didn't want to.

But even so…A suffocating sensation crept up her throat. She couldn't take dutiful obedience as far as marrying a stranger—especially one picked out for her because of his rank. Where did the princess of Arcadia end and Rose begin? If she married Prince Leo as everyone wished, she would never find out.

But her traveling companion didn't come from Arcadia,

and Natalie showed neither surprise nor disapproval at Rose's declaration. Instead, her tone was matter-of-fact as she said, "That's good, since I intend to marry him myself."

Rose blinked at her, at a loss for words.

"*You're* going to marry Prince Leo?" she managed eventually.

"Why not? Your mother was a commoner before she married your father, and so was Charlotte before she married your brother."

"I didn't mean…" Rose shook her head. She hadn't been thinking of Natalie's rank. "I just had no idea you'd been to Lanover before! Or has Leo visited the mountain kingdom? I had no idea he was already in love."

The suffocating sensation melted away, her dilemma resolved without any need for rebellion on her part. If Leo was already in love with someone else before he even met Rose, then her parents couldn't expect Rose to catch his interest. There would be no reason for them to be disappointed in her. It was the perfect solution. Thank goodness she had agreed to take Natalie to Lanover with her.

"Oh, Leo and I have never met." Natalie's unabashed words punctured the bubble of happiness inside Rose. "But I'm going to be a queen one day, like Charlotte."

Rose stiffened as she grasped the full meaning of Natalie's words.

"Are you serious? You asked to accompany me to Lanover because you want to trick Prince Leo into marrying you so that you can become a princess?"

"A queen," Natalie corrected her, again without the slightest sign of shame.

Wrath filled Rose. She knew what it was like to have

people feign interest in you because of your rank, and she wasn't going to allow Natalie to trick Leo into marriage.

She promptly informed Natalie as much. But her withering criticism made no dent in Natalie's confidence. Had she entirely misread the girl? Up until now, Natalie had seemed enthusiastic and lively—the opposite of cold and mercenary. If anything she had seemed heedless of rank—nothing like the more toadying members of the Arcadian court. That type was usually obsessed with formality and hierarchy.

Natalie's eyes flashed as she refuted the charge of trickery. "It's not as if I have an enchanted object on hand to force him to fall in love with me. I'm just giving him the chance to get to know me. If he falls in love with me on his own, then fair's fair. I don't see what's wrong with that. And I'm not mercenary at all. I have no particular interest in gold. I didn't pick Lanover because it's the wealthiest kingdom. It was the only one that had a crown prince the right age."

"The only one that..." Rose's words died in the face of Natalie's effrontery.

"What's the matter now?" Natalie demanded, and her genuine confusion struck Rose as irresistibly humorous. Were they seriously having this conversation?

"You...You're..." Her giggles were verging on the edge of hysteria, and she fought to rein them in.

When she finally succeeded—Natalie staring at her as if she'd lost her mind the whole time—she tried again.

"You might not be mercenary for money, but you're certainly pursuing Prince Leo for his rank. You can't deny that."

Natalie took her time to respond, seeming to give the charge serious consideration. "That's true. But it's not as if I want the rank so I can live a rich, easy life, or have people bowing to me all the time."

"Why do you want it, then?" Rose asked, not willing to let Natalie off so easily.

"I want to matter!" Natalie's eyes sparked, her spine straightening. "Or, at least, I want to do things that matter. Is that such a terrible thing? During the rebellion, my actions helped to change everything—not just for me but for my whole kingdom. It was incredible!" She deflated. "But I'm just a commoner girl, so it was easy for them to exile me after their desperate need was over."

"Exile?" Rose hadn't seen any hint of that. "Queen Gwendolyn brought you to Arcadia herself! She seemed genuinely fond of you."

"It wasn't Gwen who barred me from court," Natalie said. "She even argued my case to my parents. But they were convinced that the best thing for me was to go back to an ordinary life and forget about everything that had happened."

Natalie scowled out the window, but Rose couldn't help feeling some sympathy for the girl's distant parents. She could only imagine the effect of unleashing a fourteen-year-old Natalie on a royal court.

"Perhaps," she couldn't resist suggesting, "they were concerned about your obsession with becoming royal. Or is that a newer goal?"

She had been afraid the other girl might respond in anger, but Natalie grinned back at her. "The idea may have occurred to me back then, yes. But it started as a momentary dream, fueled by beautiful dresses and the excitement of the moment. It was only later that I realized that becoming royal was the only way to ensure no one could shut me out again."

Her expression had turned black, and Rose couldn't bring herself to speak her thoughts aloud. In her experience, being royal gave you less agency in your own life, not more. But at least she could feel more sympathy for Natalie now that she better understood her motivations.

"There must have been a lot of work needed to rebuild the mountain kingdom after the old queen's brutal rule," she said. "I can understand why it was hard to be excluded from that after being central to the rebellion. But that's hardly poor Prince Leo's fault!"

"You say that as if I intend to mistreat him!" Natalie protested. "I have every intention of being a delightful wife. You're supposed to love someone for who they are, and Prince Leo's rank is an integral part of who he is—as well as his future. It would be more of a disaster for him to marry someone unsuited or unwilling to one day be queen than to marry someone who wants that role. His place in the royal family is his whole future." She regarded Rose curiously. "Wouldn't you consider your rank to be an integral part of you?"

Rose swallowed and looked away, shaken. Natalie's words were too close an echo of her own earlier thoughts. How could she refute Natalie's conclusion when Rose herself had just been lamenting that she didn't know where the princess ended and the girl began?

"Yes, I suppose so," she murmured, reluctantly.

"Exactly." Natalie sounded satisfied, as if she'd successfully proved her point. "How many girls throughout history have taken one look at a good-looking young man and decided on the spot to fall in love with him? I don't see how this is any different."

"I suppose it's true that people do that," Rose said cautiously, not having considered the matter in that light. "But how many of them delude themselves in the process, only to rue that decision later? What if you don't actually like Prince Leo when you meet him?"

Natalie waved a dismissive hand. "The chances of that seem small. He's sure to be good-looking for a start—the Lanoverian royal family is famed for their beauty. And aren't princes trained to be both charming and responsible? I'm sure he'll be delightful."

"But what if he's arrogant and entitled?" Rose couldn't help pushing Natalie, fascinated by her strange way of looking at the world. Rose had lived her whole life among royalty and nobility, and yet she'd never met someone as sure of herself as Natalie. "He is a crown prince, after all."

"So is your brother," Natalie countered. "And he's never seemed arrogant. From what I've seen, he's kind, charming, and honorable. I'm sure Leo will be the same."

Rose wrinkled her nose at Natalie's description of her brother. "Don't tell me you have a misguided affection for Harry!"

"For Prince Henry? No!" Natalie sounded genuinely startled. "He's married! And too old besides. Leo, on the other hand, is only a year or so older than me. It's perfect."

"But what if you don't like him?" Rose pressed. "What if he laughs at all the wrong things and you find everything he says boring?"

Natalie wilted. "Then it will all have been for nothing." A few seconds later she straightened. "But I'm sure he'll be perfectly charming!"

"Even if you do fall in love with him, what if he doesn't fall in love with you?" Rose's eyes narrowed. "You won't be the first girl to show interest in him."

"But none of those girls are me," Natalie said, so matter-of-factly that there didn't seem to be anything to say in reply.

Rose fought another hysterical giggle. She had started the journey under a gray fog, as if a filter were obscuring the beautiful landscape around her. But the fog had lifted completely during her conversation with Natalie—the world appearing before her in a whole new way.

"I suppose there isn't anything wrong with you making the attempt," she said. "As long as you won't pursue a match unless there turn out to be real feelings on both sides." She grimaced. "That's what my parents are hoping will happen with me, after all. It's almost exactly the same, in fact."

"You see!" Natalie's face flushed, her eyes alight with fervor. "Far too many people fail at what they want in life because they don't make the effort to go out and get it. Like in my kingdom." Her voice turned dark. "Everyone suffered under that usurper for far too long because all the adults dithered instead of taking back the kingdom."

"You say it like it's that easy!" Rose cried, thinking of everything that held her back and the tasks that felt too heavy for her slim shoulders.

Natalie shrugged. "I never said it was easy. But if you truly want something, you have to be prepared to sacrifice for it. And dithering in the meantime won't get you anywhere." A scornful sound in her throat made it clear just how little patience Natalie had with dithering.

"So what's your plan?" Rose's earlier outrage had been completely consumed by curiosity. Did her audacious new friend have any chance of success? If Leo did fall in love with Natalie, it would solve Rose's problem just as effectively as if he'd already been in love with her.

Natalie's lips twisted to one side. "I'll have to see the lay of the land first. I expect my biggest issue will be getting enough time with Prince Leo. He may be closely guarded." Her eyes narrowed thoughtfully, her intense gaze focused on something far distant.

"Whereas I, on the other hand…" Rose sighed.

From her parents' gentle hints, she suspected there were similar hopes of a marriage alliance shared on the Lanoverian side. She was likely to have far more time with Prince Leo than she wanted.

A glimmer of an idea came to her. It was so outrageous that she would normally have rejected it without a second thought. But Natalie's presence was infecting her. Instead of rejecting the daring idea outright, she gave it enough space to plant itself in her mind, putting down roots before she had time to second-guess herself.

"What if we swapped?" The words tumbled out of her mouth, quivering in the air between the girls.

CHAPTER 2

"Swapped?" Natalie stared at her. "What do you mean?"

"Just for the first few days. As a...a laugh—a prank. That's what we'll tell the others when we switch back anyway. But even if we only keep it up for a few days, it will give you the chance to spend some initial time with Leo. If you truly do like each other, everything else aside, then he won't mind when you turn out not to be a princess after all. And if he does mind, then the feelings weren't real. You can treat it as a test. And if he has no real feelings for you, you have to promise you'll let the whole idea of marrying him go."

"You mean we should switch places? That I would arrive in Lanover as Princess Rose and you as Natalie?" Natalie's eyes lit with impish excitement at the idea, even as her words protested. "But how could that ever work? We don't look anything alike!"

"That doesn't matter." Rose warmed to the idea with each passing moment. "My maids are loyal to me and will stay quiet if I ask it. And I've never met Prince Leo, only his sister, Princess Beatrice. King Frederic and Queen Evangeline have visited the Arcadian court with Beatrice, but none of them are going to be at the Lanoverian court when we arrive. Now that King Leonardo and Queen Viktoria have stepped down, and Leo's parents have been crowned king and queen, all four of them are going on a tour of the kingdom to ease the transition. Almost all the senior court are going too, as well as Princess Beatrice and her cousins, Princess Violet and Princess Iris. Only the prince is being left behind. From what my parents said, I think it's a test of sorts—to see how Prince Leo performs in their absence now that he's officially crown prince. It's why my parents agreed to send me alone. It will only be a few younger members of court at the Lanoverian palace for the next few weeks."

Rose had been desperate to go alone, hoping it would ease the new feeling of suffocation that had come over her in the last few weeks.

"Only young people? Are you sure?" Natalie looked hopeful.

"I heard the Duke of Sessily will be staying—*to keep a discreet eye on the young prince.*" Rose repeated the words she'd heard from one of her father's senior advisors. "But I've never met him either, only his mother the Dowager Duchess—and despite her age, she'll be going with the tour."

"I thought you weren't willing to trick Prince Leo," Natalie's tone teased, her eyes dancing with excitement.

"This is different." Rose spoke with as much dignity as she could muster. "While I'm sure he doesn't want to be courted only for his rank, neither do I. Fooling him into calling us the wrong names for a few days is hardly a trick of any consequence." She arched a brow. "It's not at all the same as fooling him into committing his life to someone whose only interest in him is acquiring his rank."

Natalie laughed. "From everything I've heard, it's exactly the sort of prank that would appeal to Prince Leo. According to the rumors, he and his cousin, Prince Luca, spent their entire childhood getting into mischief. So he can hardly get angry at us for doing something similar ourselves."

Rose had heard the same rumors—probably more of them than Natalie had, given the mountain kingdom's isolation. And if Leo was the sort of person who liked to cause mischief but couldn't accept being on the receiving end…

"If he's the sort of person who can't take what he himself dishes out, then neither of us should marry him, prince or not," she said, warming even more to her idea. "So it really is a test of sorts." She gave Natalie another warning look. "And you do need a test, given the danger of deciding who you're going to fall in love with before you know anything about them as a person."

"That seems fair." The criticism bounced off Natalie, unheeded. "But I'm sure he'll pass the test. I don't expect to have any problem caring for Leo the person."

She seemed to genuinely believe her words. Were hearts really so biddable? If so, perhaps Rose's parents were right, and she should do her duty and pursue Prince Leo herself. She sighed.

Natalie frowned at her. "Why are you so set against

him, anyway? Given everything we've heard about Prince Leo and the whole Lanoverian family, he's likely to be an easy person to fall in love with." Her eyes widened. "Not that I'm not grateful," she added in a rush. "I wouldn't want us to be in competition."

"I just want to make my own choice." Rose looked down. "But I'm afraid of…" She let the words trail off, struggling to put her complicated feelings into words.

Rose loved her parents too much to relish disappointing them. And she loved Arcadia, too. She just wasn't sure how much of herself she was willing to sacrifice for her kingdom.

Did that make her a terrible person?

A sudden change in the air of the carriage brought her head up. Natalie was leaning toward her, her eyes pinning Rose to the seat.

"You're afraid? Has someone been threatening you?" Natalie's voice vibrated with passion. "Have they hurt you?"

Her sudden vehemence both touched and startled Rose. Natalie looked ready to run someone through at the mere thought that her new friend might be the victim of abuse.

"Is that why you've been so on edge?" Natalie demanded when Rose didn't immediately answer. "Is that why you want to switch places?" She made no attempt to wait for an answer before plowing on. "Because if so, forget a short-term ruse. We can turn the carriage around right now, and I'll sort the villain out before we go a mile further."

"Would you really?" Rose couldn't help the question,

although she knew she should reassure her friend. "And what if it's my parents, the king and queen?"

Natalie blinked, her face going blank for a moment before she seized Rose's hand in a reassuring grip and gave her a bolstering look.

"Don't worry. We'll find a way. You can count me as a friend, no matter what." She drew a deep breath. "I've helped bring down a ruler before."

"I can see how." Amusement tinged Rose's voice. "You really don't let anything overwhelm you, do you?" She squeezed her new friend's hand before pulling out of her grip, grateful for Natalie's eager defense of her. Natalie had a strange way of looking at the world, but she clearly had a strong sense of justice.

Rose stumbled through an explanation of what she'd actually meant, and Natalie sat back against her own seat. She clearly would have liked more detail, but Rose wasn't in the mood to expand on her basic words. She had never talked to anyone about her struggle to differentiate between her personhood and her role.

But as the two girls shook hands on their plan, discussing the more practical details, Rose felt an unfamiliar stirring of hope. For the first time she was going to have the chance to exist separate from her title. For the first time she might actually discover the answer to the question that plagued her.

And perhaps she could use the extra free time to find answers for her parents as well. They had sent her off with the unspoken task of falling in love with Crown Prince Leo, but there had been a spoken assignment as well—even if it was talked about in hushed voices.

It was momentous that her parents had trusted the sensitive matter to Rose alone, and she was determined not to let them down.

With her official task in mind, she reminded Natalie of the necessity of passing on any messages she might receive that were intended for Princess Rose. If Rose was going to disappoint her parents in her choice of husband, she wanted to prove herself capable in other matters at least.

CHAPTER 3

Rose examined the members of the Lanoverian court who had gathered to welcome the new arrivals to the palace. She rarely had the opportunity to study anyone so openly, but all eyes were on Prince Leo as he greeted the apparent princess.

Rose had often thought it must be freeing to disappear into the background, and so far the experience hadn't disappointed. Her earlier qualms—which had grown as they approached the city—melted back into nothingness.

Freed from the usual inane exchange of civilities, she examined the gathered courtiers without restraint. An older man stood to the back, watching the young people greet each other. From his expensive outfit, she guessed him to be the Duke of Sessily rather than a steward. But he seemed content to remain in the background—confirmation of the current state of the Lanoverian court. The young people were to be allowed a light rein.

She relaxed even further, not even flinching when Prince Luca glanced in her direction, his eyes brimming with amusement. She wasn't sure what Natalie was saying, but apparently at least one of the princes found the two of them humorous.

Did he already suspect something? If so, he certainly didn't look offended.

Natalie also glanced her way, and Rose gave the other girl a smile of encouragement. Natalie's voice rose in volume as she introduced Rose, giving her assumed name, of course.

Rose's smile was still lingering on her face when Prince Leo obediently followed Natalie's gesture and locked eyes with her. Rose froze, hit by the intensity of his gaze despite the space between them.

She had been prepared for the prince to be good-looking, but not that one glance would leave her breathless and off balance. His gaze held hers, lingering for far too long as warmth rushed into her cheeks.

He finally turned back to Natalie, and Rose could breathe again. Thank goodness she wasn't the one forced to walk at his side and receive all his smiles. Rose had already firmly decided not to fall in love with Prince Leo, and she mistrusted her instinctive reaction to him. She wasn't the sort of girl Natalie had talked about—the kind who decided to fall in love with a man because of his looks.

And she wasn't going to fall in love with one because of his rank either. But apparently after nineteen years of dutiful life, even her emotions were meekly responding as they had been bidden. Rose couldn't permit that—otherwise there really would be nothing of Rose the girl left.

Despite her defiant thoughts, her earlier calm unconcern had evaporated in the intense gaze of Prince Leo.

She had to hear what Natalie was saying and make sure their ruse wasn't blown too soon. The noise of the servants around her had grown, obscuring the words of the royals, so Rose shifted closer, trying to look inconspicuous.

She edged close enough to make out their words again and caught Leo referring to Natalie as Lila. A moment's confusion gave way to admiration as she realized Natalie had somehow produced a nickname obscure enough not to give their game away. It was a pity Rose didn't have anything similar to utilize. She didn't relish answering to someone else's name any more than Natalie did.

Should she make up a nickname on the spot? It wasn't as if anyone would know the difference. She had set out to discover her true self beneath her royal role, so why shouldn't she choose a name for herself?

She considered the possibilities. If she could be called anything, what would she choose?

Her mind remained stubbornly blank of anything except Rose. She had always liked her name.

No, she told herself firmly. *I can do better than that.*

But with every name in the kingdoms open to her, her mind remained empty. She didn't want to pick something at random and end up with a name that felt foreign and wrong.

A distant memory tickled the edge of her mind, and she seized it. When she had been very little, her grandparents had called her by a pet name—one she had nearly forgotten. But now the image of her grandmother came back to her, looking younger than she did now as she laughed with her small granddaughter. Her head had been bare on those occasions and her clothing simple enough for her to play with a young child.

Posey. She could hear the commanding voice of her grandfather softened as he called for his Rosey Posey. How had she forgotten those long ago days? She had been so young then—unaware of her duty and willing to demand that her whole family take the day off from their official duties to spend it with her.

Those moments together had been more treasured than any of the elaborate court entertainments, and whenever she had heard that nickname, she had felt like an ordinary girl—a secret person separate from Princess Rose. Rosey Posey didn't have to sit still or watch her manners for formal occasions.

Rose's family had continued to make time for her in the years since—but it was a few hours here and there, sometimes half a day, and usually only with one adult at a time. Never a whole day all together—not since she had grown too old to beg for something so indulgent.

Lost in her reminiscences, she started in surprise when Prince Luca appeared beside her. But royal habit kicked in, and her mouth curved in a smile, hiding her true feelings.

The crown prince's cousin grinned back. "With a welcoming smile like that to greet me, I don't feel banished in the least." His eyes flickered to where Prince Leo and Natalie were moving toward the palace doors.

What had Natalie said? Had she forgotten herself already and been rude to the Lanoverians? Why had she sent the younger prince away?

Or had Leo been the one to banish his cousin, wanting

Princess Rose all to himself? Apparently he was more open to the possibility of a match than she was.

She forced herself to breathe. By all accounts Leo and Luca were incredibly close, and they were supposed to be alike in temperament too. Neither of them was known for taking things seriously. She shouldn't read too much into Luca's lighthearted words.

"I'm Posey," she said boldly, holding out her hand.

He took it in a firm clasp, bending his head over it, although the brush of his lips was so light she wasn't sure she'd actually felt them.

"Did I hear wrong, then?" he asked as he straightened. "I thought it was Natalie."

Rose wrinkled her nose and laughed, affecting an unconcern she didn't feel. "Only on formal occasions. My friends call me Posey."

"I will endeavor to prove worthy of the honor, then." Even as he spoke the gallant words, his eyes strayed back to where Leo and Natalie were walking through the palace doors.

Rose turned up the intensity of her smile. Was it suspicious that both she and Natalie had immediately requested the use of nicknames? Had Rose already misstepped?

But it was too late to take back her words. It would look even more strange if she retracted them now.

Instead she stayed silent, accepting Luca's offered arm and letting him lead her toward the palace. As they walked, she snuck sideways glances at him, trying to keep her curiosity concealed. His face no longer held the hint of hidden laughter. A crease of concern marred his brow as he watched the disappearing backs of the other two.

But when he caught her watching him, the expression melted away, replaced with his earlier lurking amusement. "This visit might turn out to be more entertaining than I anticipated," he murmured.

Rose raised a brow. "Were you expecting Princess Rose to be boring?"

Luca looked back at the palace doors. "Boring is one thing she definitely isn't."

Rose barely suppressed a wince. What in the kingdoms had Natalie been saying to the princes?

Inside the palace, the air was cooler, and Rose looked around her with pleasure at the elegant, tasteful interior. Luca flagged a passing maid and gave instructions for the princess's friend to be assigned a guest room.

The maid assured him that there were always guest rooms ready and offered to take Rose to one herself. He relinquished her to the maid with alacrity, despite a fresh wave of empty gallantries. For all his engaging manner, she could tell his heart wasn't in it.

She watched him stride off down the corridor, unsure what to make of Prince Leo's closest friend. Did he suspect something or not? She genuinely couldn't tell.

"Miss?" the maid prompted, clearly impatient, and Rose shook herself.

"Sorry," she said with a conciliatory smile.

The maid nodded, somewhat curtly, and gestured for Rose to follow her down the corridor.

Unsettled by the girl's brusque manner, Rose followed silently, reminding herself that she was no longer Princess Rose. She had arrived as an uninvited—and possibly unwanted—guest.

She had thought she was sick of the empty formalities and trite civilities accorded a princess, but clearly she was more used to them than she'd realized. She hurried to catch up to the maid, determined to prove that she didn't need special treatment.

The determination stood her in good stead when she stepped into her new room, words of gratitude steady on her lips. The maid accepted them cursorily, disappearing back to whatever duties had been interrupted by Rose's arrival. Left alone, Rose acknowledged her sense of disappointment.

There was nothing actually wrong with the room once Rose recovered from the surprise of its small size. She didn't even care about the size. The most important part of the camber was the bed, and it looked perfectly comfortable with a warm coverlet and thick mattress.

But the room was dark despite the bright sunshine outside, kept in gloom due to the single small window. Rose was used to large rooms with picture windows and plenty of natural light. But this room—clearly afforded to less important guests—sat in a corner of the sprawling building, a nearby sandstone wall filling the limited view and blocking access to the bright sun beyond.

"It doesn't matter," Rose said aloud to bolster her spirits. "I won't be spending much time in here anyway. I wanted to be an ordinary girl, and that means having an ordinary room. I should be grateful they've given me a room in the palace at all."

She was grateful. Her ungracious thoughts had merely been a momentary aberration, unworthy of her new adventurous self. She wasn't Princess Rose now, she was

Posey. And Posey was delighted to have her own room in a royal palace.

For the first time it occurred to her to wonder what sort of room Natalie had been assigned in the Arcadian palace.

The bedroom door opened without warning, and she spun around, relieved to recognize one of her own maids as the woman slipped inside and closed the door behind her.

"There you are, Your Highness." The words dripped with reproach. "I thought I'd lost you."

"Here I am, Joanne." Rose gave her a coaxing smile. "But you must call me Posey for the moment. That's what I've decided to be called here, and you need to get in the habit of it so you don't slip up in front of someone else."

Joanne gave a doubtful agreement, her face clearly signaling her disapproval. But even so, Rose couldn't help the wash of reassurance at the sight of Joanne's familiar face. Princess Rose wasn't completely gone, after all.

CHAPTER 4

Rose hadn't felt so nervous entering a formal reception in years—and she wasn't even the center of attention this time. Her unobtrusive entrance hadn't been noticed by anyone.

But she had also never entered an official function as just herself. She hadn't realized that Princess Rose had been a shield to hide behind as well as a duty to fulfill.

She drew a deep breath and reminded herself to enjoy her freedom. She would only have it for a few days, and she needed to make that time count.

Natalie had arrived before her—Joanne wasn't as good at arranging hair as Donna, and Rose had dallied over her preparations, not wanting to arrive too early—but Natalie had stalled near the main entrance of the room, stuck talking to a line of courtiers. It was a familiar sight to Rose who had always needed to greet people and exchange civilities at functions. Occasionally, if she had arrived late to a ball, she would go straight to leading the dancing. But what she had never been free to do first was what she always most wanted to do…

Rose walked in a straight line toward the refreshment table. The selection of food smelled just as good as it always did in Arcadia, although some of the delicacies looked unfamiliar. Her mouth watered as she breathed in the aroma.

All too often at home she wouldn't make it to the refreshment table at all, and someone else would gallantly bring her a plate. She appreciated the thought behind the action, but she would far rather choose her own food—especially since no one ever loaded up her plate. The kitchen staff at home always knew to expect a late night visit from the princess whenever she'd been at an evening function that didn't include a sit-down meal.

When she was young, she hadn't visited the kitchen alone, and Rose had loved the stolen moments with her amazing older brother. But then he had left, and she had been on her own with her worry.

He had returned, thankfully, but he had brought a bride home with him. Rose loved her new sister, but if Harry and Charlotte were eating late night snacks, they were doing it together, without Rose. And visiting the kitchen after an event only felt lonely once she was doing it alone.

She pushed away the melancholy thoughts. She wouldn't need to go in search of late night snacks while she was Posey. She was free to choose her favorite foods from the refreshment table and fill her plate as high as she liked.

Several younger courtiers were grouped beside the table, and she smiled at them as she picked up her plate.

Their curious gazes lingered on her in response, but none of them approached her.

Awkwardness swept over Rose, and she quickly began filling her plate to cover it. For an unthinking second, she had been expecting the other guests to approach her, and that instinctive expectation only made an already awkward moment even worse. Rose had never thought of herself as socially inept, but then she rarely had to take the initiative. In Arcadia, there was always someone who wanted to talk to the princess.

But as she chose items for her plate, she calmed. It was natural that she would feel a little awkward at first as she adjusted to a whole new identity. She might not be used to taking the initiative, but she was perfectly capable of doing so. For now, she didn't even want to talk to strangers. She wanted to focus on eating, and she was glad to be free to do so.

She filled the rest of her plate with determination, her only regret that it wasn't larger.

"You'll find the food here of the highest quality," said a male voice beside her, and she turned, a smile already on her lips, glad that someone had approached her after all.

But as soon as she saw the young man's face, her smile faltered. His grin was mocking, and his eyes lingered on her overfull plate.

"I suppose the food in the mountain kingdom is very basic," he said with false sympathy. "You'll have to make the most of your time in Lanover."

Rose's eyes narrowed. She had never visited the mountain kingdom herself, but Harry and Charlotte had told her stories about it, as had Natalie. And Rose had no doubt how Natalie would have responded to the young man's words in her place.

"Oh, you needn't feel sorry for me," she said, with a sickly sweet smile. "I suppose you're too far south to have heard of the famed mountain food, but I can assure you we have excellent food—and impeccable manners."

The young man mumbled an apology, at least having the grace to look shamefaced as he hurried away. The rest of his group trailed after him, casting wide-eyed glances back at Rose as they went.

She bit her lip. From their expressions, she guessed the young man had been goaded into approaching her by his friends and was now scolding them.

She had successfully defended the mountain kingdom —as Natalie would have wanted—but her response had been more Natalie than Rose. And now she was totally alone, despite the crowd in the reception room. She wasn't making much headway—either at being herself or at making friends without the assistance of her title.

Sighing, she turned back to her food and bit into one of the pastries. A grin spread over her face. At least the food tasted as good as it smelled.

She finished the plate more quickly than was decorous, not giving a moment's thought to her appearance while she ate. It was exactly the type of moment she had pictured when she had suggested becoming Natalie for a few days.

But as she finished the last bite, she spotted Natalie moving in her direction with Prince Luca in tow. Rose hesitated, but she had no desire to get caught in conversation with one of the Lanoverian princes, especially with

Natalie present as well. One of them was bound to get muddled and do or say something suspicious.

She moved quickly away from the table, only to realize she was still holding her plate. As Princess Rose, there had always been a servant on hand to take her plate as soon as it was empty. Embarrassment filled her as she realized she didn't know what everyone else did once they had finished eating. She glanced back at the table but couldn't see any used plates abandoned there.

Her confusion mounted as she examined her surroundings as surreptitiously as possible. She couldn't spot anyone else with an empty plate in hand, but neither could she see any servants collecting them. Now that she was considering the matter, she couldn't remember noticing what others did back home in Arcadia either. While there had always been a servant hovering near her, that couldn't be true for every guest.

Two elegantly dressed young women her own age moved in Rose's direction. Was the plate in her hands getting larger? The solid weight of its awkwardness grew heavier by the second. Seized by panic, she thrust it into the base of a small potted tree and turned to stand in front of it, facing the approaching girls. Hopefully her skirts were wide enough to conceal the abandoned plate from their notice.

She pasted on her best royal smile as they stopped in front of her. While she didn't usually need to introduce herself, she knew it was the proper way to start an acquaintance, so she opened her mouth to give them her new name.

One of the other girls spoke first. "Why aren't you with Princess Rose?"

The blunt force of her words hit Rose squarely, the sound of her own name and title throwing her off balance. She blinked.

"Ah, why would I be?" She glanced around for Natalie but could no longer see her.

"Aren't you her lady-in-waiting?" the same girl asked, her brow wrinkling in confusion.

"Oh. No, I'm not." Rose should have anticipated the mistaken assumption—it was logical given she had arrived in the supposed princess's company. "I'm just a friend. I wanted to come to Lanover, and Princess Rose kindly allowed me to travel with her in her carriage."

The girls exchanged looks that Rose couldn't read.

"That was kind of her," the first girl said. "But what are you doing here, in that case?"

Rose stared at them, her thoughts frantic. She rarely found herself at a loss for words—she had been trained to fill any awkward silences with ease. But that was when she inhabited her usual identity. She wasn't used to being on the back foot in conversations with strangers.

Clearly she had severely underestimated how prepared she needed to be before arriving at an event as Natalie. She tried to force her mind to focus.

What was the girl asking? Was she questioning Rose's attendance at the royal reception? If so, Rose couldn't think of a good explanation. Rose had just assumed she was included and turned up, but if she was at the event as an extension of the princess's invitation, shouldn't she have arrived in company with her supposed royal friend?

Had attending been a misstep? Should she have stayed in her room?

Or perhaps the girl was wondering why Rose was being accommodated at the Lanoverian palace at all. And once again, Rose had no good answer. As Rose's lady-in-waiting, her presence made sense, but as Natalie of the mountain kingdom, she was merely an uninvited intruder.

Rose's training kicked in. If she couldn't answer the question being asked, she needed to reframe it to one she could answer. She would assume they were asking her why she had come to Lanover in the first place.

Except she hadn't prepared an answer for that either. And she could hardly give them Natalie's answer. She didn't want to imagine their reaction to that much honesty.

She had to say something, though. The longer she remained silent, the more awkward the moment became.

"I…I've always heard lovely things about Lanover," she said, her face flaming. "I've wanted to visit for years."

The two girls exchanged another look, and this time Rose could read it easily. They were unimpressed by her and bemused by her presence in their court.

She had never felt so lost and humiliated in her life. And she had no one to blame but herself.

CHAPTER 5

"Natalie! There you are!" The warm, confident voice of Prince Leo broke through Rose's panic.

She latched onto his voice like an anchor in stormy seas, turning to beam at him. She had no idea why he was looking for her, but she would accept any rescuer come to pull her from the mire of her own making.

Both Lanoverian girls turned to face him, their expressions transformed into welcoming smiles. Prince Leo was clearly popular within his own court.

"Ah, Lady Trina, Lady Rachelle," he said. "I see you've already met our special guest from the mountain kingdom. I've been looking forward to talking to Natalie all evening. I've been fascinated by her kingdom ever since we first established contact." He transferred his blinding smile to Rose. "I had to take care of duty first, but I'm free at last."

Her answering smile came instinctively. She was all too familiar with the necessity to put duty before interest.

"Luca tells me you prefer Posey to Natalie," he added, still giving her the smile that scrambled her thoughts.

"Yes," she managed. "That's right, Your Highness."

"And you must call me Leo, Posey," he said warmly. "Any friend of Princess Rose is a friend of my family."

Rose pulled herself together and managed a more polished response. "I appreciate your warm welcome, Leo. Lanover is already proving just as beautiful and welcoming as the stories claim. Your gardens and palace are stunning."

From the corner of her eye, she caught the look that passed between the two Lanoverian ladies. In one easy exchange, the prince had taken all the fire on her behalf. His words had extended over her the mantle of respect owed to Princess Rose of Arcadia while also establishing her as a person of individual interest. It had been very smoothly done.

Both girls were already looking at her with an entirely different type of interest. Clearly she would now be welcomed—not because of her own efforts or merit but because Leo had painted her as someone who belonged.

At the start of the evening, she might have resented that fact. But after her abysmal performance, she felt nothing but overwhelming gratitude and relief.

Leo offered her his arm. "You really must come into a quiet corner with me and answer all my questions about the mountain kingdom." His eyes twinkled down at her. "I've heard there are enormous white bears."

Rose sucked in a breath. She didn't want to get drawn into a long conversation about a place she'd never been, but she couldn't rudely reject her rescuer. Especially not when his friendly smile was already indicating to Trina and Rachelle that they were dismissed—all without breaking its warm tone.

The girls excused themselves graciously, and Rose cautiously slipped her hand into Leo's arm. His nearness was having a strange effect on her legs, but his support was reassuringly steady.

She had known the Lanoverian family were stunning—Queen Celeste of Northhelm had once been a Lanoverian princess, and Rose had seen her transcendent beauty with her own eyes. So she should have been more prepared for Prince Leo's appearance.

But she didn't think any amount of mental preparation could have inured her to the combined effect of his tousled black hair and golden skin, nor his angular jawline and cheekbones. Not to mention his height and the breadth of his shoulders, or the easy, elegant way he moved. Leo was every inch a crown prince, confidence in every line of his body, while Rose had never been more wrong-footed in her life.

No, she would definitely be better off with more distance between them—despite the anchor of his supporting arm.

When his eyes flicked to the plate stashed in the dirt of the nearby pot, she wanted to sink into the floor and disappear from sight completely. But he made no comment about the oddness of the plate's location. He merely flicked his finger, catching the attention of a nearby servant. A second small gesture directed the man to retrieve and clear the plate away.

The tightness in Rose's chest relaxed. Her embarrassment melted away in the familiarity of the subtle interaction. Back home in Arcadia, it could have been her in Leo's place, and it made it easy to guess at the thoughts behind his actions.

In his place, she would have been distressed to see a guest to Arcadia so awkward and confused. As their host, she would have blamed herself rather than blaming the guest in unfamiliar surroundings. And she would have been eager to show them that Arcadia knew how to be hospitable and to put people at their ease.

Remembering those feelings, she extended herself some grace. She had only been playing the role of Natalie for a few hours—of course she would start by being lost and confused.

Rose glanced sideways at Leo and then wished she hadn't. He was smiling down at her, and it did strange things to her breathing. She needed to rein in her gratitude. He had saved her, but he had done it because he was the host and she was a guest. He wasn't actually interested in her, and he was literally the last person at the Lanoverian court who she wanted to spend time with.

She needed to keep their conversation short and escape as soon as possible. She had already achieved the ideal outcome when Leo established her position at court. Trina and Rachelle would ensure the information about her status spread rapidly among the other young people, and she would have an easier time with any future interactions. There was no need for further prolonged conversation with Leo himself.

But when Leo tucked them into a back corner, his interest seemed genuine, rather than just a pose assumed for the sake of the noblewomen. Unfortunately, that interest was focused on the mountain kingdom, and he had a stream of questions for her. Rose could only be grateful she and Natalie had spent so many hours exchanging information in the carriage.

And Leo was no longer touching her, at least, which made it much easier to think. Gradually, her confidence returned as she managed to keep up a sensible conversation.

"Thank you for rescuing me back there," she finally said with a self-conscious laugh. "I promise I'm not usually so awkward."

"Then all the more blame lies with Lanover for making you so," he said swiftly, confirming her earlier reading of his thoughts.

"Oh no!" she said. "It's all my own foolishness."

"I suppose you must be unfamiliar with royal functions," he said politely, but she could read the curiosity in his eyes. He wanted to know how a commoner girl from the mountains had become friends with the Arcadian princess, but he was too polite to ask prying questions like Trina had done.

"I'm actually friends with Gwen," she said, remembering to refer to Queen Gwendolyn as Natalie did. "So I do have some experience of court."

She didn't mention Natalie's banishment from court because it seemed safe to assume Natalie wouldn't bring it up. And it was better for Rose to give Posey a history with court functions. She had far too much experience with them to make it easy to feign complete ignorance. Hinting now that she was used to mingling with nobles and royalty might save her if she forgot herself in the future and said something too revealing.

Leo's eyes glowed with interest at her casual mention of the mountain queen, but he didn't press her for more information.

"Given your kind words about Lanover earlier," he said instead, "I have to assume that Luca was more welcoming than Lady Trina. I'm glad we haven't entirely disgraced ourselves."

"Actually, I think Luca was more interested in Princess Rose than me," Rose said, nearly tripping over her own name. "But your welcome has been far more than I deserve." She wanted to apologize for pushing herself into the Lanoverian court in the first place, but she hesitated to bring up the subject. She still hadn't worked out an acceptable reason for Natalie's presence.

"Was he, indeed?" Leo laughed softly and added something so quietly that Rose barely caught the words. "He isn't usually so obedient."

Her brows drew together as she tried to make sense of his words, but he quickly smiled.

"I was utterly fascinated when I heard the news that a kingdom had been discovered deep in the mountains. As a child, I was always convinced those mountains couldn't be as impassable as everyone claimed. If I hadn't been a prince, I think I would have attempted to cross them myself."

Rose's eyes widened. "I'm glad you are a prince, then. You wouldn't have been the first one to disappear into the mountains and never return. A proper pass exists now, but outside of it, the mountains are just as deadly as claimed."

He smiled. "Don't worry. As a lad, I wasn't bothered by thoughts of duty, but I'm crown prince now, and far too responsible to go off adventuring."

Rose bit her lip and looked down. Was that a criticism aimed at her brother—who had done just that despite being crown prince?

Leo watched her, frowning in confusion, and she remembered that she wasn't talking to him as Rose. Of course he hadn't meant it as a slight on her brother. She had already lost track of the role she was playing.

Rose forced herself to look up and smile. "Duty can be a heavy burden, but sometimes it protects us as much as it takes from us." Her experiences in the last hour had certainly demonstrated that.

"That's an interesting way to view it," Leo said. "I've never thought of it quite like that. But as a royal, I can certainly see your point. Our duty is heavier than most, but so are the benefits we receive from our position."

Rose winced internally. She had been so eager to cover up her momentary awkwardness that she had spoken from her own experience without thinking.

"I can imagine it must be difficult," she said softly.

Did Prince Leo ever feel the way she did? Did he ever want to escape his title and his role?

"Sometimes it can be difficult," he acknowledged, his eyes warming as he smiled at her. "But this is not one of those times. It has been a great pleasure to monopolize the time of our newest guest."

She looked away, trying to fight the flush warming her cheeks. The supposed princess was a new guest as well—shouldn't he be spending his time with her?

How had she forgotten her intention to cut their conversation as short as possible? She was supposed to be enabling Natalie to spend time with Leo, not spend time with him herself.

She stood abruptly. Leo stood as well, concern in his eyes.

Rose forced a smile and dropped him a shallow curtsy. "You have been more than gracious, Your Highness."

His brows quirked, a confused smile on his lips. "Leo, please."

"Leo," she murmured in acceptance.

"It has been a pleasure to make your acquaintance, Posey." He took her hand and bowed over it in a mirror of her own formality. But unlike with his cousin, Rose had no difficulty feeling his lips against her skin—the sensation shot through every nerve ending in her arm.

She snatched her hand away. "I'll be sure to let Princess Rose know about your kindness to me. I know she's looking forward to getting to know you."

Something that could have been disappointment shadowed his eyes, but he smiled graciously and assured her that he looked forward to spending time with them both.

CHAPTER 6

Rose lay awake for some time, considering all the ways the evening had gone wrong. She just hoped Natalie wasn't angry that Rose had spent half the night talking to Leo after claiming in the carriage that she had no interest in him. She resolved to do better at avoiding him in future and finally fell asleep—only to dream of brown eyes, dark hair, and broad shoulders.

She woke early the next morning, despite the late night. During the daytime, she had bemoaned the low lighting in the room, but after her first night, she was dismayed to discover that her chamber had the opposite problem in the early morning. The thin curtains did little to keep out the first rays of the sun, and she was awake far sooner than she would have liked.

Accepting the inevitable, she rose and looked around for her tray of breakfast. There was no sign of it.

Clearly it hadn't been delivered by a Lanoverian servant, and Joanne—apparently less sensitive to light than her royal mistress—still slept in her cot against one wall.

Rose sighed. After her late night at the reception, Joanne had no reason to anticipate Rose's early waking. And apparently Natalie didn't have a high enough status for a local servant to deliver the tray. It wasn't as if Natalie was an invited guest.

Rose felt a brief moment of impatience with the mountain girl. She really was the most outrageous creature, and she'd left Rose in a difficult position as a result. Except it hadn't been Natalie who suggested they switch. So it was Rose herself who had created her own problems.

She briefly considered waking Joanne, but the maid had been carriage-sick half the way from Arcadia and had then waited up for Rose's return the night before. She needed her sleep.

"I'm supposed to be an ordinary girl right now," Rose whispered to herself. "Surely I can find the source of breakfast as easily as Joanne."

Armed with determination, she let herself out of her room, closing the door as quietly as possible behind her. Thankfully her early waking meant it was breakfast time for the servants and minor officials of the palace, and once she reached a main corridor, she was able to follow a steady stream of people to the general dining hall.

The vast room might never have been graced with a member of the royalty or nobility, but it was a pleasant space, lined with long tables and filled with the buzz of voices. Rose's spirits lifted as she smelled the food and followed the man in front of her to join the line along one wall.

Continuing to follow the lead of those ahead of her, she took a plate and shuffled toward three kitchen helpers who filled the plates of those filing past. No one asked who she was or questioned her presence. No one commented on her gown either. She'd chosen the simplest one in her wardrobe—the only one she could get into without assistance—but it was still out of place in her current company.

She did notice eyes flickering her way as she took an empty seat at one of the tables, though. Had she violated some invisible seating plan? She smiled tentatively at the older man sitting across from her, and he frowned back.

"I saw you at the reception last night," he said. "You were one of the guests." The rest of his words were implied: If she had been a guest at the royal reception, what was she doing eating breakfast with the servants?

"I saw you, too," a younger man beside him said. "When I was clearing plates. You were talking to His Highness."

"Which one?" asked a young woman further down the table, covering her mouth to giggle.

"Prince Leo," the woman across from her said before turning to Rose. "I heard you're from the mountain kingdom. And don't have any rank."

They all stared at her, waiting for her to confirm the rumors.

"I'm Posey," she said, preferring to keep her words as truthful as possible. "And I hope it's all right for me to be here. I woke early and was starving, so I followed my nose."

Several of them laughed, the tension broken, although a third man several chairs away continued to regard her with an intense look. She vaguely recognized him, her mind telling her he was a footman. He must have been present at either her arrival or the reception. Had he seen her behaving oddly? She tried not to meet his eye.

Conversation continued over the meal, but she contributed little, focusing on eating as quickly as possible. People continued to arrive, while others left whenever they finished their meal, providing a constant flow of people that made her feel less conspicuous.

Those seated near her seemed to have accepted her presence and were continuing as usual, except for the occasional glance her way or stifled comment when Princess Rose came up. Rose had the impression they were all greatly interested in the arrival of a foreign princess but were restraining themselves due to her presence. The faster she could eat and leave, the more comfortable they would be.

She wasn't the only one making them uncomfortable, though. When a new group of men arrived, almost everyone around her stood to leave, shoveling in any remaining mouthfuls as they left. Rose regarded the newcomers, but they wore a variety of uniforms and looked no different from the other servants in the room to her eye. She stopped watching them when they chose seats on the other side of the room—clearly she knew nothing about the dynamics of the servant hall and staring wasn't going to bring understanding.

Only one person at her table seemed unaffected by the latest batch of diners. The vaguely familiar footman made no move to leave, continuing to stare at her between every bite. His concentrated focus unnerved her more than the combined interest of all the others had done.

What might he have seen or overheard? Rose wracked

her brain to remember where she had seen him, and a sudden, sickening image came to her. It was true that she had seen him before and in the role of footman—but she hadn't seen him in the last two days. She had seen him at home, in her own palace. He had been one of the footmen to accompany Frederic on his last visit to Arcadia—back before he became king, when he had visited as crown prince.

She stood so abruptly that the conversation at the next table broke off. She tried to smile at the curious faces turned her way, but her features seemed to have frozen. The footman had recognized her, and any second he was going to blurt out her true identity.

Her mind emptied of every thought except to flee. Dropping her plate and cutlery in the large tubs near the door, she dashed out of the dining hall. She had been out of place in there anyway, just as she had been at the reception. She had no idea where Natalie was supposed to fit in the palace hierarchy, so maybe it was a good thing she was about to be exposed.

But as she hurried down the corridor, her mind started working again, and her steps slowed. From the intensity of the man's stare, she had to assume he had recognized her immediately. But he hadn't said anything. Something was keeping him quiet, and that meant she had a chance to convince him to stay silent.

She just had to find a way to speak to him alone. Turning back toward the dining hall, she walked slowly, considering her options. A middle-aged woman came through the doors, giving her an odd look as she hurried away in the opposite direction. And then the very person occupying Rose's thoughts stepped out, looking down the corridor first one way and then the other.

As soon as the footman caught sight of her, he broke into a jog, heading toward her. Clearly he had followed her out.

"We need to t—" she began.

He seized her arm and pulled her through a plain wooden door into a large storeroom, shutting the door behind them just as fresh voices exited the dining hall. He immediately dropped her arm and took several steps back.

"My apologies, Your Highness." He bowed low.

"So you do recognize me," she said ruefully. "I wasn't so quick to recognize you."

He bowed again. "I'm honored you remembered me at all, Your Highness. It makes this conversation a little easier. I, of course, recognized you as soon as I glimpsed you yesterday."

Rose's brows rose. "You already recognized me yesterday? How many people have you told?"

"None," he said simply, and her brows rose even further.

It sounded too good to be true. Was he planning to blackmail her or something? She wanted to stay as Natalie a little longer, but she wasn't committed enough to the role to allow someone to blackmail her over it.

"I've been trying to work out how to manage a private word with you," he said. "I needed to establish the purpose of your charade before I could work out how to proceed. So you can imagine how pleased I was when you turned up in the dining hall this morning without a maid in tow." The intensity returned to his eyes. "Are you in danger, Your Highness?"

"In danger?" She stared at him, taken aback by the direction the conversation had taken. "Not as far as I know."

He relaxed. "I was concerned you might have been forced to assume a different identity for your protection. If that was the case, then I could have gotten you safely out of Lanover and back to Arcadia without anyone knowing your location or route."

"You could have?" Rose asked, finally guessing at the footman's true identity.

"Certainly, Your Highness," he said. "I wouldn't have needed direct instructions to know my duty in that circumstance."

"Instructions," she said slowly. "I'm guessing you don't mean from Prince Leo."

CHAPTER 7

The footman gave Rose a tight smile. "As you've guessed, I'm an agent of Aurora, and I have instructions to make contact with the Arcadian princess on her arrival. I had detailed plans on how to achieve that, but they were all thrown into chaos when I realized the girl in the princess's suite wasn't actually the princess."

"You have a message for me from Aurora?" Relief swelled inside Rose. She'd hoped to contact Aurora's network herself, but she hadn't had any idea how to go about it.

A possibility occurred to her. "Have you already found the thief?" She looked at the man hopefully.

She wanted a chance to take on some responsibility—to prove her competence. But it was far more important that the situation be successfully resolved, even if that was without her involvement. The potential damage to Arcadia was too great to take her personal feelings into account.

"I'm afraid not, Your Highness." The footman cleared his throat. "We've been pursuing the matter through unofficial channels only, as requested by your parents. And that has put limits on our progress."

Rose nodded. Her parents didn't want to risk word getting out that a thief had successfully stolen an official Arcadian seal. The news could do incredible damage to people's confidence in Arcadia—across the Four Kingdoms and even beyond.

It was bad enough when the thief had been loose in Arcadia, but tracking him down grew harder when he headed south into Lanover. Word of his passage had reached the Arcadian royals through Aurora's network, and Rose's parents had immediately taken their daughter into their confidence. Rose's visit to Lanare had already been planned, and they wanted to take advantage of her presence in Lanover. It was much better to have the search overseen by one of their own, rather than admitting the truth to the Lanoverians.

Privately, Rose had even feared the Lanoverians might keep the seal for themselves if they were the ones to recover it. But having met Leo, it was hard to reconcile that possibility with the reality of the man. She could no longer imagine him doing something so underhanded toward an ally.

"Do you have more information on the thief's where-abouts, at least?" she asked, desperate to hear there had been some progress in the investigation.

The man hesitated. "We've received conflicting reports. There is some concern that he may have managed to infiltrate the palace itself and be working here."

"In the palace?" Rose stared at him. "Is that possible?

Surely that would make him obvious to you and your fellow agents."

The man shifted, looking even more uncomfortable. "Ordinarily so, yes. But there has been an influx of new hires lately, and there is a possibility he could be among them. However, that isn't our only lead. Other rumors place him in the city. Our network has been investigating a forgery ring operating out of Lanare for some time, and we believe it possible—even likely—that the thief has linked up with them."

"A forgery ring?" Rose's eyes widened. That sounded like a much more substantial operation than a single thief.

Unease shot through her. Her parents had charged her with helping Aurora's network find and apprehend the thief of the seal. Surely this agent didn't want her to get involved with the investigation into an entire forgery ring? She didn't feel comfortable doing something so large-scale in someone else's kingdom. The last thing she wanted was for her involvement to create an international incident.

The footman picked up on her concern, continuing quickly. "Of course we have constant surveillance on the red door, but we haven't yet managed to identify the man in question."

"The red door?" she asked, bewildered.

"My apologies, Your Highness. We've identified a building that we believe is being used by the forgers, and it happens to have a red door. We've fallen into the habit of referring to it that way."

Rose nodded, trying to look wise in the ways of spy networks.

"What do you need from me, then?" she asked, hit by a new worry.

She didn't want to get overinvolved, but neither did she want to be excluded completely. And the more she thought about it, the more likely it seemed that her parents had never intended her to get involved with the investigation at all. They had probably planned for her to do no more than pass messages back and forth between Arcadia and the agents and—hopefully—to carry the seal safely back to Arcadia once it was retrieved. But she wouldn't be able to take any pride in the seal's recovery if her only role was as courier.

She clenched her teeth. She might not be one of Aurora's agents, but she was more capable than that.

"We need you to report every detail when the thief contacts you," the footman said. "Even the smallest thing might turn out to be of import."

"You're expecting him to contact me?" Rose stared at the agent, completely distracted from her earlier thoughts. "The thief knows I'm here?"

The man hid a smile. "The whole palace and a large part of the city knows you're here. Our information suggests that the man has ambitions to make further use of his theft by using it for blackmail."

Rose's eyebrows shot up. So it wasn't the footman who meant to blackmail her but the thief.

"He'll most likely contact you by letter," the man said. "Although your charade may complicate things. I'm not sure if he knows your appearance."

"Given he's spent time in Arcadie, there's every chance he does," she said grimly.

Her one consolation was that the thief would be unlikely to expose her. Doing so would only call attention to himself, so he would probably keep his mouth shut.

"You haven't received any strange communications since your arrival?" the footman pressed.

Rose shook her head. "Nothing at all. But I'll check with Natalie."

The footman nodded. "You can contact me again any time by simply coming back for another meal in the dining hall. If I see you there, I'll find a way to follow you when you leave."

Clearly he wasn't expecting her to continue eating at the hall regularly. Rose hadn't been the only one to notice she was out of place.

"That sounds simple enough," she said. "I'll return if I receive any sort of communication from the thief."

"Thank you, Your Highness." The footman bowed and hurried from the room, not lingering for small talk.

Rose lingered in the room for several more minutes, not wanting to be seen exiting a storeroom too soon after a footman. When she finally did leave, she had to stop another servant and get directions back to her room.

By the time she arrived back, she felt as if she'd lived at least half a day already. And yet Joanne was only just stirring.

Her maid insisted on helping her into a more elaborate gown, as well as rearranging her hair. Rose submitted meekly to Joanne's ministrations. Joanne had been her maid the longest, which was why she had been the one assigned to stay with Rose, despite Joanne's lingering sickness the day before.

At least the long sleep had proved restorative, and the maid talked brightly about her plans for the day. Those plans all seemed to revolve around acquainting herself with the workings of the palace, so Rose suspected she would find a breakfast tray ready when she woke in future. Rose might be masquerading as Natalie, but her maids hadn't forgotten what they felt was due her dignity—as evidenced by Joanne's disparaging comments about the room.

"I'm sorry you have to put up with these conditions alongside me," Rose said meekly to Joanne, and the older woman's eyes snapped up.

"Really, Your Highness! How can you even think such a thing? Obviously I'm concerned for your dignity."

Rose laughed. "And yours by extension. Don't think I don't know how it works. But don't worry. I—and you—will be back to our proper place soon enough."

Joanne put the last pin in place in Rose's hair and stepped back.

"In that case, Your Highness, I'll be about my business for the day." She paused. "Unless you're needing me for anything else?"

"No, no, continue with your plans." Rose didn't bother to mention her own plans. She didn't need Joanne's help to track down Natalie.

As it turned out, the task proved even easier than she had imagined. No sooner had Joanne left than the door sprang back open. Natalie tumbled into the room out of breath and shut the door firmly behind her.

Rose blinked in astonishment, trying to gaze past Natalie to the closed door. Was someone chasing her? She held her breath as she waited to see if the door would spring back open. Who had the temerity to chase the supposed Arcadian princess through the palace?

But the door stayed firmly shut, and no footfalls were heard in the corridor outside. Rose raised both eyebrows in a question, but Natalie wasn't looking at her.

Whatever had driven Natalie into Rose's room at such speed had been forgotten as she gaped at her surroundings, her expression slowly turning guilty. Rose suppressed a smile as she imagined the room Natalie must now be occupying. She'd known the rooms would be different, but the contrast must have been even greater than she'd imagined.

Rose said nothing, however, waiting with some interest to see how Natalie would respond. Given Natalie's firm belief in her future royal position, Rose hadn't expected to see so much guilt in the girl's face.

"Sorry about the room," Natalie said simply, sounding genuinely contrite.

Rose's heart softened toward the outrageous girl, and she waved off the apology. She was far more interested in what had brought Natalie to her room in the first place— and just as Rose was wanting to see her.

"Is everything all right?" she asked.

"Yes, I just…wanted to check on you." Natalie's halting words fell limply to the floor between them.

Rose slowly raised an eyebrow, and Natalie looked away uncomfortably. Was she still feeling guilty about the rooms? Or was something else unsettling her?

"I hope your room is to your satisfaction," Rose tried, hoping to prod the other girl into further speech.

Natalie's whole face lit up in excited animation. "Oh

yes, it's stunning! The view is incredible…" Her brain caught up with her words, and her voice dwindled, her face twisting in another apology.

Rose suppressed a laugh. "I'll look forward to seeing it when we switch back places."

A new possibility occurred to her. Had Natalie come to suggest they swap back immediately? The evening before hadn't gone to plan, but it was only the first function. Rose's mind was already spinning with ways to follow up the agent's disclosures, and she would be much freer to do that without her royal rank drawing attention.

Thankfully, Natalie didn't take the opening Rose had unintentionally provided, merely murmuring agreement about the rooms.

Rose considered her next words carefully. Natalie, who wasn't even Arcadian, knew nothing about the theft, so she would need to question her subtly.

"You've remembered what I said about not getting into any political discussions, right?" she asked, echoing the words she'd used previously in an attempt to obscure her real point of interest. "And about passing on any letters or notes you receive for me?"

She watched Natalie closely, but the girl's earlier discomfort over the rooms still lingered in her expression, making her hard to read.

Natalie nodded. "Yes, of course. I remember." A note of irritation crept into her voice. "I can promise it was nothing but inanities last night. All except one conversation which went on forever and was just a constant stream of reminiscences about your parents and grandparents."

Rose straightened. There had been a whole group of

people at the reception who knew her family? What had Natalie said to them? Had she exposed her ignorance?

"Don't worry," Natalie said quickly. "I just smiled a lot and said almost nothing, so I don't think I gave anything away."

Rose slumped back down, relieved. Not that she could complain after her own haphazard performance with Lady Trina and Prince Leo.

When Natalie left in almost as much of a whirlwind as she'd arrived in, Rose took a few minutes to catch her breath. They had made it through the first night without being exposed and would apparently be maintaining their ruse a little longer.

But the conversation with Natalie had provided no insight about the missing note. Would one be arriving in the next day or two, or had the thief changed his mind about blackmail?

CHAPTER 8

While Joanne spent the day exploring the portion of the palace that belonged to the servants, Rose spent it exploring the extensive palace gardens. She didn't even think about what Natalie was doing with her day until she caught sight of the other girl from a distance. Natalie was also walking through the gardens, but she was firmly ensconced in the middle of a group of young courtiers, and their path was taking them out of the palace grounds.

Was Rose supposed to be among them? The thought was clearly belated—if she was, it was too late now. She continued to wander through the greenery as she pondered the broader issue. Did the prince's public welcome the previous evening mean she should consider herself invited to all other court events?

It was easy to imagine Natalie seizing the opening. If they hadn't swapped places, she would have leaped at the chance. But Rose hadn't become a commoner for a few days so she could spend her time hanging on the fringes of royal society.

But what did she want to do instead? Back in the carriage, the question of what she would do as Natalie had seemed distant and unimportant. But now it had become both immediate and unanswerable.

What she wanted to do was find the items stolen from Arcadia. But her only assignment from Aurora's agent had been waiting on a letter that might never come. Was there really nothing more active she could do to help?

Unfortunately, determination proved insufficient to provide an answer. Even as she slipped into bed that night, she still hadn't come up with anything useful. But she couldn't spend all her time wandering in the gardens alone —that was even less appealing than joining the court functions as Posey.

Despite her frustration, she slept well and woke to breakfast on a tray. She ate beside her one small window, enjoying the quality of the food, if not the view.

As she savored the last bite, she considered her options. She could visit Natalie's room and find out the court's plans for the day. Even if Natalie was already gone, one of the maids would be there and would certainly share the information with Rose. But the idea held no appeal.

Neither did more aimless exploration. She had enjoyed it the day before—the Lanoverian royal gardens were well worth a day's visit—but one day had been enough.

That left the city. The footman had spoken about a forger's circle based in a building in the capital. Rose didn't have the skills to infiltrate the forgers, but she'd like to at least see their headquarters for herself. And if she should happen on a clue while she was there...

She didn't stop to consider how many buildings in Lanare had red doors—she didn't want to know the answer. Instead, she once again dressed in her most practical gown and left the palace.

With each step away from the building, she felt a little freer. She had made her own decision and was acting on it —without needing to explain and justify herself or submit to the fuss of an entourage. Just Rose and her own two feet.

"Posey!" The voice drifted across the garden, pulling her to a surprised stop. She turned, unable to see the speaker at first and unable to guess who might be seeking her.

Leo emerged around an ornamental hedge and strode toward her, moving just short of a run, although he wasn't out of breath.

"Are you heading into the city?" He smiled down at her. "Do you want a guide?"

"That would be lovely." Her mouth answered before her mind could caution her to refuse.

With Leo at her side, she wouldn't be able to actively pursue the forgers' building. The most she would be able to do was keep a watch for any red doors. But he looked so light and carefree that she couldn't bring herself to reject his thoughtful offer. He had managed to escape his duties for a brief excursion, and she wouldn't be the one to stand in his way.

He fell into step beside her, and she eyed him from the corner of her eye. At the welcome reception, he had looked every inch the royal prince. Now, however, he wore ordinary clothes, distinguished only by the excellence of the cut.

Not that anyone could ever think Leo was *ordinary*—not with his face and bearing. But he looked far closer to it than Rose would have imagined possible. Her own simple gown appeared elaborate by comparison.

He caught her peeking and grinned. "Are you shocked? I'm guessing the royals in the mountain kingdom aren't so casual."

She shook her head and laughed. "Not shocked. But perhaps…mildly surprised?"

He chuckled. "We've always been less formal here than in the other kingdoms. It's harder to be ceremonial all the time when it's this hot."

"Lanover must be very relaxed indeed if the crown prince is permitted to wander around the city without any escort at all."

"Except for one mountain girl?" he quipped, and she reluctantly laughed.

"I don't think anyone would consider me much protection."

"Thankfully we aren't likely to need protection. Even in my father's day he was allowed to ride into the city without guards or grooms, so he can't complain when his son does the same."

"Fascinating," Rose murmured.

Arcadia wasn't the most formal of the kingdoms, but she had always been accompanied on trips outside the palace grounds.

"In truth, I should be spending the day stuck behind my desk," Leo confided. "But I caught a glimpse of you from my chamber window and made a hurried change of plans. I'm glad I caught you before you left the grounds." He took a deep breath of the fresh air. "Now if anyone asks, I have a good excuse for abandoning my duties."

He grinned at her as if it was a stratagem hatched between them—a conspiracy for two. She couldn't help smiling back.

Since there was no wall around the palace, there were no gate guards to note their prince's exit, and no one questioned them as they left the grounds and entered the city. But Rose had to suppress the instinct to look over her shoulder. She kept expecting someone to hurry after them and prevent their escape.

Leo laughed, and she realized he was watching her again. "You look as if you're escaping from prison. I promise we don't lock up our guests in Lanover."

"I'm glad to hear it," she said lightly, her royal training keeping the internal wince from showing.

Leo began a light commentary as they walked, pointing out buildings of either architectural, historical, or social note, and making her laugh with his anecdotes of the mischief he had managed in the city during his childhood —always with his cousin alongside.

Somewhere amid the laughter, Rose forgot the itching feeling that they might be pursued and reclaimed at any moment. Leo wasn't supposed to be there beside her, but he was easy company.

"My own childhood was sadly ordinary by comparison," she said.

"Even under the rule of the usurper queen?" Leo asked, clearly surprised.

Rose bit her tongue. "I wasn't at court then, of course," she said quickly. "My parents were only assigned to their current liaison role after the throne was restored." She tried to steer the conversation away from Natalie's childhood. "But it's interesting to see the differences between Lanover and Arcadia. It makes me wonder what the other kingdoms are like."

At least Natalie had visited Arcadia, so Rose had an excuse to talk about it.

"When I was a child," Leo said, "my parents visited Arcadia and brought back a painting of its palace. My sister and twin cousins pined for at least a week. Beatrice kept insisting that was what a real palace looked like, and the twins tried to convince Father to build several extra stories on top of ours." He grinned. "They were convinced we needed a tower or two at the very least."

"But the Lanoverian palace is beautiful in its own way," Rose objected. "The style is different, of course, but the gardens are incredible—and you've still got a view, even without any towers."

Leo laughed. "You don't need to convince me. I wouldn't change it for anything." He smiled fondly back in the direction of the palace.

"What made your sisters and cousin change their mind? Or do they still prefer other palaces?"

"Thankfully it was the same year the twins begged their parents to commission beds for them that would stack on top of each other. They received the beds as a birthday gift, but when the temperature increased they discovered the flaw in their plan. Iris insisted it was too hot to get to sleep on the top bunk and ended up sharing Violet's bed below.

After that, they accepted the reality that heat rises, and they gave up asking for extra levels for the palace."

"Princesses on bunk beds like soldiers?" Rose laughed. "Your aunt and uncle must be very accommodating."

"The twins can be very persistent," Leo said dryly. "But Aunt Tillie had the good sense to design the beds so that the top one could be removed and used as a normal bed alongside the bottom one. So the furniture didn't go to waste, even after the idea of stacked beds was abandoned. I believe they still use them today."

"How sensible," Rose said approvingly. She hoped she was equally flexible when she had her own children one day.

A few moments passed in silence before she gave a small sigh. "I wish I'd had a twin."

Her aunts were twins, and each of them had given birth to a pair of twins themselves. But her young cousins lived across an ocean.

Leo grinned. "There's nothing quite like it."

She raised an eyebrow, and he added, "My aunt and uncle have always lived at the palace with us, so Luca has been as good as a twin to me. And, of course, Iris and Violet always had each other. Poor Beatrice used to feel left out."

Rose's brows drew together in sympathy. She had wished countless times in her life that she had a sister of her own. For the most part, Harry had been an excellent sibling, but it wasn't the same.

"Don't feel too sorry for her." One side of Leo's mouth quirked upward. "Those three were thick as thieves, and the dynamics were always shifting. At other times, Violet was the one to feel alone and excluded. I always found it hard to follow, but my mother told me there are stages to these things."

Rose laughed. "There usually are." She had always adored her older brother, but she could remember certain ages when he had been far less accepting of a younger sister following him around everywhere.

"It would have been nice to grow up with a collection of cousins," she said wistfully.

"I certainly have more than I know what to do with," Leo said cheerfully. "But thankfully they don't all live in Lanover."

"Do you ever get together with all of you?" Rose asked, wondering how the practicalities of that would work, given how far the Lanoverian royal family had spread.

"Only once," he replied with a laugh. "We all gathered in Northhelm, and at the end of the visit, our parents decreed never again. According to Father, the host kingdom might not survive a second such occurrence."

"But now you're a serious crown prince who *always* puts his responsibilities first," she said with mock solemnity. "It's quite sad, really."

He shook his head. "Surely *usually* should count. Think how dull I would be if I did nothing but work."

She huffed out a disbelieving laugh. It was impossible to imagine Prince Leo ever being dull.

Only later, when she was lying in bed, did Rose remember her plan to look for red doors. With Leo's distracting company, she had forgotten all about her original intentions for the day.

And on sober reflection, she had to admit the distraction had been a good thing. Her original plan had been ridiculous. Even if she had somehow stumbled on the right building, she was never going to find a clue lying around outside it. She might even have caused trouble for Aurora's agents. The spy network might be able to surveil a building covertly, but any clumsy attempts by Rose would only draw the forgers' attention.

The impromptu walking tour had been a far better use of her day. With Leo's help, Rose had gotten a taste of the city, and of Lanover, that she wouldn't have managed in a whole string of court functions. She felt sorry for Natalie, stuck at the official festivities instead.

Rose stilled in her bed, guilt creeping over her at the thought of Natalie. Rose had forgotten more than her search for the red door. The whole point of taking Natalie's place had been to avoid Leo and let Natalie spend time with him in Rose's stead. Rose had failed completely.

She could have refused Leo's escort, or at least invented an excuse to return to the palace after the first couple of hours. Had he intended to join a court event that afternoon only to get caught up with her for the whole day instead? How could she have let that happen?

But when she had imagined spending time with Prince Leo as Princess Rose, she had pictured stilted court interactions—conducted under duress and in front of an interested audience. Their day in the city had been nothing like that.

Leo had joined her by his own choice, knowing nothing of her true identity. He had volunteered his time as a friendly gesture to an interesting visitor—not because he'd been instructed to pursue a match for the sake of an alliance. He was probably enjoying a final few days of freedom before taking up those *responsibilities* he had mentioned.

She wrinkled her nose, her mood souring at the thought. He was currently smiling at Posey and showing her around the city—he had even promised to complete the tour over the next few days. But soon he would be courting 'Rose' without any emotion behind it.

The thought tainted the image of him in her mind, and she told herself she should avoid him in future. But when the next day arrived, she changed her mind. She should finish the tour of the city, at least. She wanted to get to know Lanover, and no one knew it better than its prince.

At the end of the week, Rose had utterly failed to avoid Leo, but she had successfully dodged most of the court functions. Natalie wasn't happy about it and had made her promise to attend the planned ride along the coast—one of the few events actually hosted by the crown prince himself. Rose agreed, knowing she had no excuse to avoid it—Leo had already given Posey a direct invitation.

Not that she read anything into that. The prince probably wanted her there to bear witness to the beginning of his courtship of the princess. He had probably started worrying that Posey might get the wrong idea, given all the time they had been spending together.

And that was a good thing. Leo was supposed to be spending his time with the so-called princess.

Rose resolved to dedicate herself to Natalie's cause, promising that she would not only attend but also help maneuver their positions so that Leo rode beside Natalie. It was the least Rose could do after monopolizing so much of the prince's time—a guilty secret she hadn't yet confessed to Natalie. The court had been running the false princess ragged with their events, and Natalie hadn't had the energy to monitor Rose's whereabouts as well.

The riders gathered in front of the palace, and a nameless groom approached Rose with a sedate mare for her to ride. She thanked him despite her internal dismay. The horse looked like a boring ride—especially compared to the quality of mount provided for Natalie. But it didn't matter. Rose wasn't joining the ride for her own benefit.

Despite her internal monologue, she couldn't help a

rush of pleasure as she swung into the saddle. It had been too long since she had been on horseback. She hadn't even realized how much she missed it.

She also couldn't help noticing Leo's excellent seat. He was clearly as comfortable on horseback as he was roaming the city on foot. Not that Rose was surprised by that. Of course a prince would have been trained to ride. She really shouldn't be looking.

She determinedly resisted the impulse to sneak glances at him, focusing her attention on Natalie instead. But Natalie's attention had been caught by someone on the other side of the group, far from Leo, and Rose couldn't see who it was through the mass of shifting riders and horses.

Rose moved her horse closer to Natalie's, positioning herself ready to nudge Natalie toward Leo's side. At least the other girl's attention had returned to its intended target, and she was watching Leo with a fixed attention that belied her earlier distraction.

Rose frowned. That wasn't much better than her inattention had been. Natalie needed to relax a little if she didn't want to scare Leo away!

They rode through the city in single file, but Rose managed to secure the place between Natalie and the rest of the riders, with only Leo in front of them. When the road widened, she would do whatever it took to keep her horse as a barrier, holding back the rest of the riders until Natalie had taken the spot at Leo's side.

When they finally left the city behind them, Leo glanced back. His pace slowed as the road widened, leaving space beside him. For half a second, Rose thought his eyes had turned in her direction, but she didn't stop to check.

With subtle pressure, she sent her mare dancing, effectively blocking the road. When she had the mare back under control—a far easier task than getting the placid animal to prance in the first place—Natalie was in place beside Leo, and Prince Luca was trotting his horse forward to ride beside Rose.

She watched with satisfaction—it was definitely satisfaction!—as Natalie and Leo conversed, not even noticing her own companion's silence. But when Leo glanced back in their direction, Luca startled her by speaking.

"My cousin seems to have remembered the princess's existence." Luca's words carried a note Rose couldn't read, although she had always prided herself on reading people well. Was he trying to give her a hint?

"It's only natural they should spend time together," she said stiffly, unable to think of anything else to say. Conversation with Luca was nothing like the easy flow of words when she was with Leo.

The ocean drew closer, the road sloping downward as it angled toward the coast. Before long, only a thin stretch of grass separated them from the sand.

"There isn't anything natural about this," Luca declared, once again making her start. She scrambled to remember what she had said to provoke such a response, but he didn't seem to notice her confusion, continuing on in a strong voice. "On a glorious day like this we should be galloping along the sand, not plodding sedately along the road."

Rose's brows contracted. She didn't disagree with him exactly, but she wasn't about to go galloping away from the rest of the party—even if her horse could be goaded into a gallop, which was doubtful.

But Luca wasn't looking at her. He guided his mount forward without another word in her direction. Riding along the grass verge, he came up beside his cousin, and Rose caught the challenge he called to Leo.

"Race along the beach, Leo?"

Leo didn't respond, but Luca wasn't abashed, laughing and calling out again.

"Don't let Lila hold you back." He used Natalie's chosen nickname. "I'm sure she thinks she can beat us both." He shot a look in Natalie's direction, his eyes sparkling.

Rose's frown deepened. Natalie wouldn't go racing off across the beach any more than she would, but Luca should have known better than to suggest it. He was placing her in an awkward position.

But when Luca directed his horse onto the sand with a whoop, Natalie responded instantly, racing after him with calls of foul play. The two of them sped off across the sand as startled murmurs broke out from the double column behind Rose.

Leo was watching the two racers with a speculative look in his eyes, but when he caught sight of Rose's expression, he glanced quickly at the rest of the group.

"My cousin is right," he called in a loud voice. "It's far too nice a day not to venture down onto the beach."

He turned his own mount toward the sand, although he moved at a sedate pace. Rose's mare fell into place beside him, Natalie's departure forcing her to take the position she had intended to avoid.

Once on the sand, they followed after Natalie and Luca, although they kept to a much slower pace than the racers.

Leo chuckled. "Perhaps I was wrong about the differences between Lanover and Arcadia. Their princess seems just as relaxed as any Lanoverian."

Rose's eyes flashed to the distant figure of Natalie. She had finally stopped her headlong dash and was in the process of shaking her hair completely loose of its pins.

Leo wasn't the only one to have noticed either. The voices of the courtiers continued to rumble in surprise and interest, and Rose ground her teeth together. Natalie had promised not to bring Arcadia into disrepute while acting in Rose's place. Clearly Rose should have been keeping a closer eye on her.

She urged her mare forward, using all her skill to coax the sluggish horse to action. Leo kept pace easily, and they reached Natalie and Luca ahead of the others.

Rose angled her mount away from the two princes, approaching Natalie and whispering frantically to her, an edge to her words.

"Quick, put your hair back up before the others reach us and get a proper look at you! What were you thinking?! Princesses are supposed to behave with more decorum!"

Natalie's entire demeanor changed, her bright smile crumpling, and Rose felt a prick of regret. But she wasn't scolding Natalie on Rose's own account—she was doing it for the sake of Arcadia. If Natalie had gone for a private ride with a couple of friends, it would have been one thing, but she was at an official court event.

"I've lost most of my pins!" Natalie whispered, sounding frantic. "I'll never be able to get my hair respectable again."

Rose glanced at the approaching riders and then toward the princes. She could hardly get down and start searching in the sand for the lost pins. She'd never find them.

Leo responded to the appeal in her eyes, urging his horse toward them. "If you'd like to return to the palace, Lila, I can escort you there myself."

Rose suppressed a stab of irritation as she realized how completely Natalie had disrupted the outing. She should have been feeling relieved instead since Leo's suggestion would give Natalie some time alone with him.

But Luca spoke quickly, cutting into Leo's plans. "Don't forget you're the host today, Leo. You can't leave. But I can escort Lila back if she wishes to go."

Natalie hesitated, but she really had no option other than nodding acceptance of his offer. The two of them wasted no time in heading toward the grass, riding away just as the first of the other riders approached.

"We should ride on," Leo said softly. "Cover any awkwardness."

Rose nodded hearty agreement, and they both urged their mounts back into movement. She felt bad about sending Natalie and Luca away, but the prince had been foolish in issuing his challenge, and Natalie had been just as foolish in accepting.

The frustration and guilt slowly seeped out of her, the soft breaking of the waves eroding her tension until the tightness across her shoulders eased. She gazed across the sparkling water. It was impossible not to relax in such a gorgeous setting.

"My apologies, Posey," Leo said stiffly, his manner taking her by surprise. Apparently the beauty around them wasn't having the same relaxing effect on him.

She gazed at him, her brow creased. "What do you have to be sorry for?"

"I'm apologizing on behalf of my cousin." Leo sighed. "I hope Princess Rose won't be too upset."

"I'm sure she'll recover," Rose said shortly, then sighed herself, softening. "I'm sure Prince Luca will look after her."

"Yes." Some life returned to Leo's voice, and his eyes sparkled. "It does seem so, doesn't it?"

Rose shot him a confused look, but he was smiling toward the ocean, his bearing already lightened considerably.

"Do you often ride down to the beach?" she asked.

"Not often enough," he said absently before looking at her and smiling properly. "And never in such appealing company."

She looked away quickly and told herself he must be thinking of the departed princess. As she should be. It was Natalie who was supposed to be spending time with Leo, not Rose.

CHAPTER 10

Rose paced up and down her room, but it was too small for the movement to be truly satisfying. With a huff of frustration, she pushed open the door, striding down the corridor instead. Her steps lead her deeper and deeper into the palace, but she didn't stop. Her mind needed the movement as she tried to sort out her thoughts.

She was letting herself get distracted. Already she had been Posey for longer than she'd intended, and yet she hadn't used the time to achieve anything for Arcadia. She hadn't even managed to avoid Leo. She certainly hadn't held up her end of the bargain and enabled Natalie to spend any time with the crown prince.

Distracted and moving too quickly, she walked straight into someone. Bouncing backward, she nearly lost her balance completely, only just managing to save herself from falling. Looking up, her apology died on her lips.

"Natalie?" The name slipped out before her brain caught up, and the other girl's eyes widened at her slip.

Natalie shifted slightly. "I'm sorry," she said in a rush.

Rose stared at her blankly. She'd been the one to walk into Natalie, and she'd also been the one monopolizing Leo's time. Why was Natalie the one apologizing?

"I shouldn't have forgotten myself and gone racing off like that," Natalie said, and memories of the unfortunate incident at the beach came flooding back. Rose had been so focused on herself that she'd forgotten Natalie's behavior.

Dread filled her. Had Natalie been looking for her? Was she about to say they needed to swap back? Rose wasn't ready, but how could she justify disagreeing? She had been the one to lecture Natalie at the beach, telling her she was disgracing Arcadia.

Rose scrambled to think of something to say that would stop the next words before they came out of Natalie's mouth. She failed.

"I'll do my utmost to be more mindful in the future," Natalie said. "I don't want to do anything to embarrass you or your kingdom."

Rose blinked. Oh. Apparently Natalie wasn't going to insist they switch back after all. The tightness in her stomach unknotted, and she didn't try to analyze the strength of her reaction.

"I'd already forgotten about it," she said truthfully. "I think Leo smoothed things over sufficiently with the others." She hesitated. "I'm sorry you haven't had much chance to spend time with him."

"I wasn't sure if you'd noticed," Natalie said glumly. "But he barely attends court functions, so there hasn't been much I can do." She sighed. "I suppose he has a lot of duties while his parents are away."

Rose nodded sympathetically, still recovering from her momentary panic. "If there's anything I can do to help..." she said vaguely.

Natalie only nodded acknowledgment, and Rose tried not to feel relieved. She would have liked to cheer the other girl up, but her one attempt to manipulate matters in Natalie's favor had ended in disaster. She wasn't exactly eager to rush back in.

What she really needed to do was stay in the background more effectively than she'd managed so far. Leo had to be looking for opportunities to start courting the supposed princess.

The two girls stood awkwardly for another moment before Natalie murmured goodbye and drifted away. Rose picked her own direction at random, choosing a path that would lead her away from the mountain girl. Natalie seemed like she wanted space.

Running over the short conversation in her mind, Rose barely noticed as she passed the dining hall and moved further into the servant's domain. Only when the sound of raised voices penetrated her consciousness did she look up and take stock of her surroundings.

She hadn't heard raised voices in the Lanoverian palace before, so she frowned toward the source of the disturbance. But whoever was venting their anger—a woman by the sound of it—was out of sight around a corner.

Rose hurried forward as the shouter continued to disparage her victim's abilities, person, and even parentage. She rounded the corner to find two women standing over a younger woman. The object of their vitriol was cowering, her head down and her back to the corridor wall, reacting to their words as if to physical blows.

"Excuse me!" Rose strode forward. "What do you think you're doing? There can be absolutely no excuse for such abuse!"

The younger woman kept her eyes lowered, but the other two turned to Rose, both their eyebrows shooting up.

"And who are you to be telling us what to do?" The shouter asked stridently. "It's our job to train this new recruit. There's some as need a firm hand—if they're not to prove themselves a burden to the rest of us hardworking folk. I'll thank you to keep your nose out of someone else's business."

Rose drew herself up. "I'm—" The words faltered and died in her throat.

As a visiting princess, she would have had no direct authority over these women, but they would still have respected her position and her words. As Natalie, she had no authority whatsoever.

The woman laughed. "That's what I thought. And we've no more patience for meddlesome interference than we have for lazy maids." She glared at the young woman.

Rose swallowed. The two aggressors looked on the verge of physically attacking their victim, and Rose couldn't stand by and let that happen. But she was smaller than both the older women, and she doubted her ability to successfully intervene.

She looked around, but if there had been anyone else nearby, they had long since fled. Uncertainly, she stood her ground, not sure what to do but unwilling to leave.

The second woman eyed her and muttered to the other. "Come on. I don't want to miss my hot meal for the likes of her." She turned her glare on the young woman, but the poor girl's eyes were still trained on the floor.

The first woman snorted but made no protest, allowing her companion to lead the way back toward the dining hall. Rose watched them go, not releasing her sigh of relief until both women had disappeared around the corner.

As soon as they had done so, she stepped tentatively toward the younger woman. "Are you all right?"

The woman finally looked up, although she appeared torn about whether or not to speak.

"Thank you," she finally whispered. "But you shouldn't get involved."

Rose bit her lip. Was the woman worried on behalf of Rose or because she was concerned about potential reprisals from the other women?

"It's not all right for them to treat you that way," she said. "Have you talked to the housekeeper?"

The departed women might be more senior than the new recruit, but the palace housekeeper would be many steps above them all in the servants' hierarchy. She and the steward were responsible for all the inside palace servants.

"Talk to the housekeeper?" The young woman finally showed some animation, looking up at Rose with big eyes. "How could I?"

"Of course you could," Rose said firmly. "It's her job to set the tone for how the palace is run and how the servants treat each other. She certainly shouldn't be allowing that kind of bullying."

She put a gentle hand on the girl's arm, but it only made

her flinch and pull away. A horrible thought occurred to Rose, and she seized the woman's sleeve, lifting the material enough to reveal the start of a bruise.

She sucked in a breath. "Did one of those women do that to you?"

The younger woman winced. "No, they're loose enough with their words, but neither of them get physical. This was my first trainer." She gave a sad sigh. "I must be very bad at my job." She wrapped her arms around herself. "But I can't afford to lose it."

"That's appalling." Fury burned in Rose's chest. "You have to report whoever did that."

"I did." The woman looked back at the floor. "That's why I got a new trainer."

Rose relaxed a little. "And your abuser was kicked out of the palace, I hope."

The woman looked swiftly back up. "Oh no. She didn't hit me, or anything. Just grabbed me a bit roughly."

Rose's eyebrows shot up, her anger returning. "Roughly enough to leave bruises!" She took a calming breath, trying to gain control of her emotions. The woman in front of her hadn't done anything wrong, and Rose's intensity might upset her further.

"Is there no one else you can talk to?" she asked, more calmly.

The woman shrugged. "It's not so bad. At least my new trainer only uses her words." She cleared her throat. "I need to get to the meal too." She left, not meeting Rose's eyes and not saying goodbye.

Rose watched her go, her hands clenched into fists.

Some action had been taken on the woman's behalf, but it hadn't been nearly enough. She claimed that it was *only* words, but she had flinched before the verbal assault as if it had been blows. No wonder she couldn't perform effectively. How long before she crumpled under such callous cruelty?

Rose walked slowly back toward her room, speeding up as she passed the open door of the dining hall. She had no desire to look at anyone inside. How many of them were victims and how many aggressors? If the culture of the palace was bad enough that such open abuse was happening, there had to be further abuse taking place where Rose couldn't see it.

What sort of housekeeper allowed such behavior? What royal family permitted it? Did Leo know what was going on in his own palace?

Doubt gnawed at her. Leo himself had said his family were far more relaxed than the royals of other kingdoms. Relaxed enough to be careless of the well-being of those under their care?

But it was difficult to reconcile such an idea with the image of Leo. His stories had been full of mischief but never cruelty or mistreatment of others. And the locals in the city had seemed to respect—even love—their royals. Surely they would resent them if the royals routinely allowed such terrible behavior to flourish.

There was only one thing to be done. Rose would have to raise the issue with Leo directly. If he was ignorant of what was going on, Rose needed to open his eyes.

Without her royal rank, she could do nothing directly.

But she wasn't totally powerless—she had access to the crown prince. She would have to hope it was enough. Because it turned out her new role could be as constricting as it was freeing.

CHAPTER 11

Rose's anger insisted she march straight off in search of Leo. But while she wasn't officially Princess Rose, her royal training still screamed at her. If she was going to accuse another royal of running their own palace poorly and failing in their duty to their servants, then she needed a strong case. A single incident could be easily dismissed. Rose couldn't let the matter go, but neither did she want to be the one causing an international incident instead of Natalie.

So she waited, and she watched. For the next several days, she lurked around the areas of the palace most frequented by the servants, even lingering near the guard barracks and the gardeners' headquarters.

The problem wasn't as widespread as she had initially feared, but neither was it isolated. She witnessed a footman harassing a young errand boy, three guards threatening a groom, a washerwoman hitting her subordinate, and a number of people yelling at those below them in the hierarchy. And if she had witnessed that much happening in the open, there had to be more happening in places she couldn't see. It was enough to make her case.

She reached the decision outside the gardeners' building and hurried back toward the palace, considering where she was most likely to find Leo so late in the day. Her route took her past the remains of a court event, where a team of gardeners were busy packing away several archery targets.

She slowed her pace on instinct, trying to listen in without being noticed as she had been doing for days. One of the men was talking loudly enough to be overheard, grumbling to his companion about having so many extra tasks. He seemed particularly irritated by the lanterns he had already set up in the greenery outside the windows of the main reception room.

"Bad enough we have to do it whenever there's a ball," he said. "Now they want it for evening receptions as well! And that's on top of packing up this lot." He nodded toward the targets.

His companion grunted. "You're paid for your time, ain't you? If you ask me, you wouldn't be happy if you didn't have something to complain about. So maybe the steward is trying to do you a favor with all these orders."

His companion protested loudly as Rose's steps took her out of earshot. She had forgotten about the evening reception. Leo would be in attendance which meant he would already be in his rooms, preparing for the event. And she could hardly accost him in his bedchamber.

She hurried back to her own room. "I need to get dressed for an evening reception," she announced as soon as she stepped inside.

Joanne jumped to her feet, eager. "You're swapping back?"

"What? No." Rose began to strip off her daytime gown. "I'm just attending the evening reception tonight."

Joanne sighed. "Well at least that's something, I suppose. The court has been putting on all these events for your entertainment, and you've hardly attended a one!" She gave her princess a reproving stare, and Rose wondered what her maid had heard.

Had there been talk about the strange visitor from the mountain kingdom who had started lurking all over the palace where she didn't belong? If there was, it was too bad. What Rose had been doing was important. And if the Lanoverians thought Natalie odd, it was no more than the girl deserved. They'd be even more offended if they knew her real motivations in traveling to Lanover.

Rose entered the reception room in a rush, on the lookout for Leo. But she hadn't been wading through the crowd long when musicians appeared and struck up the lively strains of a dance tune. Rose paused, distracted. There was going to be dancing? There hadn't been at the last reception.

"Will you dance, My Lady?" a smooth voice asked from beside her.

She blinked at the good-looking young courtier holding out his hand toward her, her brain faltering as she tried to remember his name. She was almost certain they had been introduced before.

"Ahh…" she said intelligently.

She didn't want to dance, but neither could she think of a reason to say no. And while her mind whirled, her body reacted instinctively, accepting the outstretched hand. At home, as Princess Rose, she always tried to accept as many dance requests as possible and to give a polite explanation for any she turned down. When you were royalty, it was important not to create unfounded rumors about royal disfavor—and even more important not to create enemies for the crown.

Thankfully, her unnamed partner danced well, and Rose's feet moved to the familiar patterns without much conscious thought on her part. It left her free to continue her visual search for Leo.

He swung past her, a Lanoverian noblewoman in his arms. Rose frowned. Where was Natalie? If there was dancing, Leo should have opened it with the princess. Rose knew Natalie was in the crowd somewhere because she had caught a brief glimpse of her when she arrived.

She relaxed into her own dance as well as she could, knowing she would have no hope of talking to Leo until the dance ended. But she couldn't stop herself from continuing to keep an eye out for both Leo and Natalie as the steps took her around the dance floor.

When the song finally wound to a close, releasing Rose, she lost no time in hurrying toward Leo. If she didn't catch him quickly, he would already be dancing with Natalie, and she would have to wait again.

But when she caught sight of Leo's tall frame, he was alone and moving toward her.

"I'm glad to see you're here, Posey." His smile made her insides glow. No wonder the people of Lanover loved their royal family—if Leo alone had so much power, she could only imagine the combined effect of so much beauty.

She shook herself. "I need to talk to you."

"Perfect." He held out his hand. "Dance with me. It's the only way we can ensure we won't be interrupted."

She opened her mouth to suggest they step outside the reception room instead, but her rebellious hand once again moved on its own. She looked down at it, already enclosed in his fingers, and back up into his smile.

He glanced once toward the musicians, and they began a new tune—this one a waltz. Leo's arm circled her, pulling her closer to him as his hand tightened around hers.

Her feet skimmed over the floor, barely needing to touch the ground as she floated into the dance. Leo maneuvered them expertly around the floor, bringing out the best in her. Had she ever danced so well before?

"I was beginning to worry," he said lightly as their bodies moved in perfect, synchronized harmony. "I've barely seen any sign of you for the last few days."

Reality crashed back around Rose, bringing her feet firmly to the ground. She wasn't supposed to have her head in the chandeliers, floating around the room because Leo was holding her close. She was supposed to be having a difficult conversation—one that was likely to become awkward, if not downright hostile.

She drew a deep breath. "It's true that I've been distracted, Your Highness."

"Your Highness?" Leo's brows rose. "What's this?"

"I've noticed a situation of concern, and I've been gathering information before approaching you about it. So I'm not speaking to you as Leo, but as crown prince of Lanover. So I should address you as such."

His brows lowered, but he didn't look angry yet—only wary and concerned.

"That's perceptive of you to understand the difference," he said. "Not everyone understands what it's like to be a royal."

Rose flushed, having once again misstepped without realizing it. But she couldn't allow herself to be distracted from her purpose.

"It has come to my attention," she began, "that an unhealthy culture has taken root in some parts of the palace community."

Leo's brows shot back up, his arm around her tightening. "Have the courtiers done something to offend you?"

She shook her head. "It's not me that has been—is being—mistreated."

"I would like to think no one under the palace roof is being mistreated." His voice was light, although his expression was not.

Rose nodded eagerly, relieved at the words she had been expecting—hoping—to hear from him. "Yes, I thought surely you would feel that way!" Her words came more quickly, and she had to struggle to keep her volume down. "The issue is among the servants. I've witnessed some appalling behavior between them."

"Fights, do you mean?" he asked cautiously.

She shook her head. "No. Not fair ones anyway. I mean mistreatment from senior servants toward those subordinate to them." She quickly outlined the instances she had witnessed. "Those are all incidents I witnessed myself, just by looking, so there must be more going on out of sight."

He cursed softly under his breath, and the harsh words

had the unexpected effect of making her relax. Leo was clearly taking this as seriously as she had hoped he would.

"What is that man doing?" he growled.

"Do you mean the steward?" she asked carefully. "I was wondering about the housekeeper myself. I suggested a mistreated maid speak to her, and the girl couldn't fathom doing so. At home, our housekeeper meets every new recruit personally and makes sure they know her name and face and that she is the one with primary authority over the servants. So they all know they can go to her if someone is mistreating them."

Leo sighed. "Our housekeeper is a very experienced woman, and she would certainly not condone the behavior you've described. But Mrs. Frost has been suffering from a protracted illness and has been out of commission for at least a couple of months now. She's still bed-bound as we speak, unfortunately."

"Oh! That explains it, then," Rose murmured, reconsidering the girls' words.

But the housekeeper's illness only explained why the maid couldn't go to her. It didn't explain how such a terrible culture had grown up in such a short frame of time. Had it already been lurking under the housekeeper's eye without the royal family noticing?

They reached the end of the dance floor, and Leo spun them around without faltering, smoothing out his expression for the watching eyes. Rose tried to do the same.

"The problem will have come from the steward," Leo said grimly. "Unlike Mrs. Frost, he's new. He came highly recommended, but if this is the culture he builds..." Leo shook his head.

The picture finally came into focus in Rose's mind. It had been an unfortunate convergence. The king and queen had stepped down, handing the throne to their oldest son, Leo's father. The change of ruler would have initiated a huge change in the workings of the palace, and in the midst of that, the established housekeeper fell ill.

"Did the old steward retire alongside your grandparents?" she asked.

Leo nodded, appearing pleased at her quick understanding. "He's even older than they are, so he was past due for retirement."

The decision was understandable from the old steward's perspective, although it had turned out to be unfortunate timing for the palace. The new steward had brought in a harmful new culture just as the new king and queen were most distracted.

King Frederic and Queen Evangeline's decision to undertake such a large tour suggested their attention had been focused outside the palace, on the rest of the kingdom. They must have assumed the palace would continue to function as it always had until they settled into their new roles and could attend to it.

Not that the new steward could be personally and directly responsible for all the poor behavior. But there would always be a few bullies ready to exploit any opportunity given. And the new steward had created that opportunity.

"My parents were excessively busy in the short time between their coronation and leaving on the tour," Leo said, still spinning them around the dance floor. "But they left me in charge, and I should have noticed." His face was lined with self-recrimination.

"But you can't be everywhere at once," she said quickly, unable to help responding to the suffering on his face. "And I'm sure none of the servants would have behaved that way in your presence."

She faltered. She certainly didn't blame him for not seeing it himself, but…

"Is there really no one who would report the situation to you?" she asked hesitantly. "Someone in a position to notice what you cannot?"

Leo grimaced. "The pile of reports on my desk is worryingly high." He glanced at her and then quickly looked away. "Several urgent matters came up, and I've been more distracted than I should have been. It's quite possible there's a report on the matter that I haven't read yet."

"It sounds like an unfortunate convergence of factors," Rose said. "And it's by no means all your fault."

"But I'm the one who ultimately has authority," he said. "So, at the end of the day, it is my responsibility."

Rose pressed her lips together, unhappy. She couldn't deny the truth of his words, but she hated having caused him so much distress.

When she looked up at him, he was looking down at her, a new light in his eyes. "I didn't notice, but you did. You're not even from Lanover, and yet you not only noticed but brought it to my attention. That took courage."

Rose flushed. "Once I'd seen it, I couldn't do nothing."

"No. I can see that," he murmured, pulling her a little

closer than the dance demanded. "And I promise that I'll do my part now. You can trust me with this."

CHAPTER 12

Rose hadn't doubted Leo's words, but even so, his swift action took her by surprise. As did the note that arrived with her breakfast tray. She hadn't thought he would include her in the process.

"What does the note say?" Joanne asked, trying—and failing—to sound uninterested. "I heard it came directly from the crown prince."

"He's scheduled some interviews today," Rose said absently, her thoughts focused on his message. "He wants me to sit in on them."

"He wants you to sit in on interviews?" Joanne's tone, sharp and confused, penetrated Rose's awareness, and she glanced up.

"Is there a problem with that?"

Joanne frowned. "I suppose not. It just seems a little unusual. Shouldn't he take you walking in the gardens or something instead?"

Rose laughed. "He's not courting me, Joanne. He's just...

resolving a situation that should never have happened in the first place."

She folded the note and tucked into her breakfast, making short work of the meal. "I'll want..." She tapped her finger against her lips, considering. "My blue gown with the white detailing. It's not too ostentatious but still has a regal air. I don't want anyone questioning why I'm there."

"But why are you there?" Joanne was still frowning, although she obediently fetched the dress.

"I'm a witness," Rose said shortly, not willing to go into any more detail.

Leo had honored her by inviting her to join his interviews with various staff members, and she refused to let Joanne's wariness bring down her mood.

"I'll want my hair up in a twist as well," she added.

"Should I fetch Donna, Your Highness?" Joanne asked.

Rose sighed. "It's Posey at the moment, remember? You need to keep up the habit. And you'll do a fine job with my hair, I'm sure. You're getting almost as good as Donna these days."

Joanne smiled. Her look said she knew Rose was flattering her, but she appreciated the gesture all the same. And Rose's efforts worked since her maid stopped sighing and tutting under her breath.

Rose left her room early, but she was glad of the extra time since she needed the help of a footman to find the designated interview room. In the end, she arrived only a few minutes before the specified time, sighing with relief as she let herself into the room and found only Leo inside. The first interviewee was yet to appear.

"You came!" Leo smiled at her broadly, and she smiled back.

"I didn't expect you to include me. I'm honored by your trust."

"You're the one who noticed there was a problem, not me." He hesitated. "I invited you partially because I want you to see for yourself that I'm taking the issue seriously. But I'm also hoping your observations might be of assistance. Please don't hesitate to speak up if you notice something."

Rose flushed slightly and nodded. "Is the Duke of Sessily coming?" she asked, before remembering to wonder whether Posey was supposed to know that the duke had been left to keep an eye on the prince.

If her words were a slip, though, Leo didn't seem to notice. He merely grimaced and sighed.

"It's been so quiet—on the surface at least—that he left to deal with an issue on one of his estates. He'll be back in a few days. But there's no way I'm leaving this until then."

Rose nodded, and Leo looked like he was about to say more, but the door opened and two clerks came in, escorted by a senior guard. Leo nodded to the new arrivals, and they all took up their places—the guard at attention just inside the door, and the two clerks along one side of the table.

Leo gestured for Rose to sit across from the clerks, placing them on either side of him while the single chair across from him sat empty for the interviewee.

A tentative knock came on the door only seconds later. Leo called permission to enter, and a nervous looking woman appeared. Rose would have guessed her to be about fifty, and based on her outfit she appeared to be one of the more senior palace servants.

The woman took the indicated seat, and placed her hands in her lap, her wide eyes on Leo.

He smiled. "Thank you for coming, Hannah. It's come to my attention that the housekeeper's long illness, while already unfortunate, must also be greatly impacting the workload of the servants below her. I want to remedy that."

The woman's demeanor changed instantly, her shoulders relaxing and her face becoming more animated. Clearly she had been braced for an accusation of some kind and was relieved at the direction of the prince's words.

"Oh yes, Your Highness! There's bound to be an adjustment when a new steward is appointed, but Mrs. Frost would have seen us through. It's been chaos without her! The maids keep coming to me with problems, but..." Hannah spread her arms in a hopeless gesture. "The other senior servants are helping, of course, but there's bound to be confusion and conflicts, and—" She hesitated.

"Please speak freely," Leo said encouragingly. "I value your insights."

"I don't have the authority to discuss matters with the steward as an equal, Your Highness," she finished in a rush. "Mrs. Frost could do so, of course, but we're all doing our best to shield her. Her situation has been very fragile." She bit her lip, looking on the verge of tears.

Rose leaned forward and handed her a handkerchief. Hannah took it with a startled look and a murmured thank you.

"You must be very worried about her," Rose said softly.

Hannah dabbed at her eyes. "I wouldn't have made it to where I am today without her. She took me under her wing when I first arrived. She knows how to walk the line —a firm rein and a soft word. That's always been the way she's run the palace."

"But that's changed recently?" Leo watched her closely.

Hannah hesitated again and then nodded. "In the past, if anyone persisted in unprofessional behavior, they were dismissed. But now we're stuck just moving people around. I've shuffled my girls around when requested, but if we're going to send someone away, it has to be approved by either the housekeeper or the steward."

Leo nodded. "That's intended as a protective measure for the staff. It's one thing if someone is dismissed for unprofessional behavior, but we don't want someone dismissed because their superior takes a dislike to them."

Hannah gave a final sniff and put down the handkerchief, leaning forward as her voice grew impassioned. "It's been a fair system in the past, but that was when we had both a functioning housekeeper and a steward—and just ones, at that."

"The new steward isn't fair?" Leo kept his voice level and free of emotion.

Hannah sat back, her face paling as she realized what she'd said. Then she drew herself up, a determined look on her face.

"No, he's not. He's from southern Lanover, and he brought some of his own people with him. He favors them most of all and other southerners next." Her expression twisted. "He's always saying us northerners need a bit of strengthening. He says the palace will be stronger when we're all strong. But in my experience, that just means—"

When she hesitated again, Rose finished for her. "Enabling bullies."

Hannah threw her a look. "Exactly, miss. I see you've encountered it before."

"I learned all about what happened between Rangmere and Arcadia before I was born. Rangmere has long held similar values to your steward, and they almost invaded Arcadia because of it. Queen Ava has been working to change those elements of her culture ever since she ascended the throne, but it's not an easy thing to do when the attitude is so entrenched. It's taken her decades."

Leo threw Rose a startled look, and Hannah blinked. "Oh yes. I think I heard something about Rangmere once."

"That is not, however, part of Lanover's culture," Leo said. "And my parents have put great effort into uniting the different areas of Lanover. I know I speak for them when I say that the new steward's attitude does not align with that of the crown or the kingdom as a whole."

"He's very organized," Hannah offered, willing to be more gracious now that her complaints had fallen on receptive ears. "He keeps on top of his administration tasks, and he has some innovative ideas on how to manage work shifts." She sighed. "But it's hard to implement them when the workforce is in constant conflict."

"Can you give us specific examples?" Leo asked. "As many details as you can remember, please."

Hannah glanced uneasily at the clerks, both of whom were poised and waiting, pens ready.

"Please speak freely and don't feel any alarm," Leo said.

"We must keep accurate records, but your name won't be disclosed to anyone in your own hierarchy." He paused slightly, giving his words extra weight. "Either above or below."

Hannah nodded, but she still looked nervous, and Rose realized for the first time why Leo hadn't started by summoning a direct victim. It would have been unfair to ask them to gather the courage to tell him everything.

Hannah, however, found her words and poured out a stream of stories, big and small. In a couple of the more extreme cases, she had gone to the new steward personally to request dismissals. He hadn't approved them.

When she finally finished, Leo had one last question for her. "Did you make any attempt to approach the royal family with your concerns? I read all the reports on my desk last night, but I didn't see one from you." His tone was level without any hint of accusation.

Rose looked at him, startled. Had he slept at all? He looked as immaculately presented as usual, and if he was tired, he wasn't letting it show.

Hannah flushed. "I considered the matter, but with Their Majesties away…"

Leo's eyes flickered, his mouth twisting slightly in a wry look.

"I see. Thank you for your honesty. You may go. If you don't hear of any action straight away, don't be alarmed. I need to start by gathering information, but my family will be setting things right—including reducing your workload back to a more manageable level."

She bobbed a curtsy and thanked him, her eyes shining with hope. Clearly Hannah trusted his words. She believed that the royal family would deal with the problem—further confirmation that this wasn't a habitual problem in the Lanoverian palace.

When the door closed behind her, Leo looked at the silent guard and the two clerks, his face stern. "You were all selected for your record of discretion, and I trust you'll use that discretion now. We can't have any leaks regarding the source of our information. People will know Hannah was summoned for an interview, but I intend to interview many people over the coming week, and I won't allow any stories to circulate about who reported what."

All three nodded.

"Please return after lunch for the next interview," he told them, and they filed from the room, leaving behind the records the clerks had transcribed.

As soon as Rose and Leo were alone, Leo sighed, and leaned back in his chair. "It's going to have to end in the dismissal of the steward. I can see that already. But I can't do that in my parents' absence without thorough records and multiple consistent accounts."

"What will you do about the people he brought with him?" Rose asked.

Leo ran a hand over his face. "They'll probably have to go, too. It's clear they're causing trouble."

Rose hesitated. "It certainly sounds like some—possibly even most—are doing so. But you can't dismiss people only because of association."

Leo groaned. "You're right, of course. But Hannah gave us plenty of names, and I'm sure more will come out in the interviews that are still to come. We can limit dismissals to those who are named."

"And what if someone names someone else out of jealousy or spite? Are we going to hold criminal investigations to prove the claims?"

Leo's frown deepened, revealing the hints of tiredness on his face. But Rose couldn't let the issue go. As a child, she had stuck close to her brother as much as possible, including joining him in the training given direct heirs. Their grandfather had always stressed the necessity to act with utmost fairness whenever possible. *Resentments can build and fester*, he used to say. *And if the abscess grows big enough, it will destroy a kingdom.*

"Do you really think criminal investigations are the answer?" Leo's tone told her he didn't agree, but he waited to hear her response.

She shook her head. "The palace is already unsettled. You're working to reduce the chaos and restore order, but a host of petty investigations—most of which will struggle to find definitive evidence—will only make everything even more unsettled."

"So you would choose to dismiss only the steward?" Leo watched her with curiosity, as if he was trying to puzzle out her thoughts.

"I would start with him. He's responsible for the overall running of the palace and the well-being of all the staff under his care."

"And I'm in authority over him," Leo said. "You could argue that I'm the one who's truly responsible. Do you think I should step down too? Or my father, perhaps?"

"You're forgetting one very important difference. You didn't know what was going on, and the moment it was brought to your attention, you acted. Your steward, on the other hand, has done the opposite. He was the one to actively foster the harmful culture, and Hannah herself reported bringing it to his attention. He did nothing. He is the one who holds responsibility for what's happened, not you."

"And you think dismissing him will be enough?"

Rose shrugged. "Probably not. But if you choose his replacement carefully, and install a temporary housekeeper until Mrs. Frost recovers, they can make it clear what sort of behavior is expected among the servants—and what behavior will not be tolerated. Make it clear to every servant—down to the newest scullery maid—that they can go directly to the housekeeper or steward with any complaints."

Leo grinned wryly. "They would be inundated."

Rose reluctantly smiled. "Probably. But if every accusation is investigated, it would soon discourage frivolous complaints. There are almost certainly some among the servants who have been encouraged in bullying behavior under the current steward but who would modify their actions to meet the new standards rather than put their positions at risk. Those who can't—or won't—exercise restraint can be weeded out after the steward has left, using complaints that are fresh and easier to investigate."

She narrowed her eyes, considering. "If I were in your place, I would probably assign a team of dedicated investigators—people with relevant skill and experience—who could follow up any complaints under the direction of the housekeeper and steward. They'll be kept busy at the beginning, most likely, but as the old culture is reestablished and any troublemakers are weeded out, complaints should die back down to a normal level. Some people adapt themselves to whatever culture surrounds them. Even if they have behaved poorly in the past, they might never make trouble again."

"And you think they should go unpunished for their past behavior?"

Rose sighed. "In an ideal world, perhaps not. But removing a large number of servants at once will hugely increase the workload of the ones who remain. You would end up punishing the innocent as well."

Leo shook his head. "How much time did you say you've spent with Queen Gwen?"

Rose's eyes widened. She had completely forgotten her role as Natalie.

Thankfully the question seemed to be rhetorical, however, as he continued without waiting for an answer. "I knew it was a good idea to include you. You already understand the situation so clearly after only one interview. You must have plenty of experience with how palaces operate."

Silence seemed the safest option, so Rose kept her mouth shut.

"Will you sit in on the rest of the interviews?" Leo asked.

"I'd like to," Rose said. "If you're sure it's all right for me to be here. I'm not from Lanover."

Leo smiled at her. "Maybe not, but I trust you. And it's good to have an outside perspective." His expression turned wry. "And you're the one who brought the problem to my attention—it's a little late to hide Lanover's weak underbelly from you."

"Did you get any sleep last night?" Rose asked, unable to

help herself. "Maybe you should rest before the next interview begins."

Leo laughed, but it wasn't a humorous sound. "A bit of exhaustion is no more than I deserve. There may not have been a report from Hannah on my desk, but there was one from the stable master. He's been in his position even longer than the old steward and taught me to ride my first pony, so he had the confidence to contact me directly. But when I saw his name, I prioritized it to the bottom of the pile, thinking any issue with the stables could wait for my parents' return if necessary."

"A ruler doesn't always make the right decisions," Rose said, repeating another of her grandfather's favorite sayings, "but his true measure is shown in how quickly he acknowledges and rectifies his mistakes."

Leo's face softened, and he smiled. "You're more gracious to me than I deserve, Posey."

"Or maybe you're harsher on yourself than you deserve," she responded promptly, and he laughed.

"Perhaps." He glanced at her. "I actually ordered lunch to be delivered here. You'll join me?"

Rose hesitated only a moment before nodding. They could talk strategy while they ate, so it was really only an extension of the meeting. Refusing would be silly.

CHAPTER 13

*R*ose didn't even bother coming up with an excuse for agreeing to eat with him the next day, or the days after that. The series of interviews continued all week, covering a wide range of both indoor and outdoor staff. The various accounts painted a consistent picture, and after the first two days, Rose half-expected Leo to cancel the remaining interviews. But the prince didn't relent, driving himself hard as he assembled a comprehensive report that would satisfy even the most exacting monarch.

And as the days drew on, Rose realized he was doing more than compiling a case against the current steward. Leo's skillful questioning drew out one name consistently above the others, and she wasn't surprised when the man in question was called in on the final day of interviews, the second to last of all.

Leo asked him a very different set of questions from the ones he had asked the others, and as he reached the final question, he smiled. "If asked, would you be willing to step up and assume the role of palace steward?"

The man's eyes widened. Clearly he hadn't realized where Leo was leading. For a moment, he sat silent. Then he cleared his throat, his voice gruff as he responded.

"I would be honored to serve the royal family and the palace in any way requested."

"Good." Leo smiled with satisfaction. "I will be in contact with you again soon."

The man left the room looking dazed, and Leo grinned. "That will make things easier," he said to no one in particular, and Rose nodded.

Everyone had agreed that there was nothing to fault in the current steward's organization, and relieving him of his post without a replacement would only have replaced one type of chaos for another.

But everyone's smiles fell away as the final interview began. The current steward swept into the room, seeming unaware of what awaited him. He bowed in Leo's direction, his execution perfect for their comparative rank, but something in his manner lacked the true warmth of respect. Or did it just look that way after all the stories they had heard about the man?

But whatever his feelings toward Leo, Rose certainly wasn't imagining his supercilious smile as his eyes skipped over the guard, the clerks, and Rose herself. Clearly he considered them below his notice, his confidence unshaken despite the prince's strange behavior in interviewing palace staff all week.

However, it was equally clear that Leo had been expecting the steward's attitude. The prince's expression didn't falter as the steward failed to satisfactorily answer any of the complaints or take any responsibility for the culture he had fostered. And when he had finished answering Leo's final question, the prince sent a silent message to the guard by the door. The man opened the door promptly to allow two more guards inside—guards who had clearly been waiting ready. Leo delivered the steward's dismissal, and the man was still sputtering and protesting as the guards escorted him from the room, the door guard trailing behind the trio watchfully.

A sigh of released tension filled the room. The clerks packed up their final records with alacrity, presenting the folders to Leo and leaving. The prince just sat there, rubbing a hand over his eyes.

"That's settled, then," he said. "I hope Father approves."

"He will," Rose said firmly, although she had little personal experience with King Frederic. "You were firm and decisive but more than fair. You couldn't leave the situation to worsen until your parents' return."

Leo nodded slowly. "That's true." He gave a single chuckle. "They wanted me to try my hand at ruling in their absence, but I don't think they expected me to do anything as dramatic as dismissing the palace steward and hiring a replacement."

"They'll approve," Rose repeated. "And your servants will be grateful to you. Thankfully you have a large staff. The senior servants like Hannah will make sure that anyone who was victimized is separated from their persecutors while we wait to see who causes trouble in future."

"That was an excellent suggestion on your part," Leo said approvingly.

"But I never thought of using the interviews to find a replacement steward. I didn't even realize what you were doing for an embarrassingly long time."

Leo grinned at her. "We make a good team."

He stood, stretching after all the hours spent sitting bolt upright. Strolling around the table, he leaned casually against it, smiling down at her.

"I think you surprised some of your people this week," Rose said, remembering some of the looks that had been sent Leo's way. "In a good way, I mean."

He smiled ruefully. "I hope so. I suspect some people were concerned when my parents announced I would be taking their place during their absence. I think I've always been fairly well liked—if I do say so myself." He chuckled. "But most people know me for my past mischief-making with Luca. They think of me as a good-natured trouble-maker and little better than a child. But I'm not a child any longer, and I want to be taken seriously."

Rose looked up at his broad shoulders. No one with eyes could think of him as a child. But she managed to catch the words before they escaped, saying instead, "Well, you've just dismissed the palace steward and chosen his replacement. I don't think anyone will fail to take you seriously in future."

"I didn't do it for that reason," he said quickly.

She placed a hand on his arm. "I know that. And so does everyone else. You just did what needed to be done. I'm glad your own people now know they can respect you." She sighed. "But I hope you don't find every week as demanding as this one. It's exhausting!"

Leo laughed. "I certainly hope not. Especially since I

haven't truly changed—not underneath. The same mischievous lad is still there, I just have proper responsibilities now as well. I have to believe it's possible to be a good crown prince—and one day king—while still finding enjoyment in life."

"Not just possible but essential," Rose said with conviction. "Without some lightness, the heaviness of the crown would crush you. Monarchs should still be able to laugh."

"Exactly! I want to use my position to help my people, but it's only reasonable I should get to have fun sometimes as well." He grinned down at her, and she laughed.

"What sort of fun do you have in mind that's acceptable for Crown Prince Leo?"

"Actually," he said, his voice dropping and taking on a husky note, "lately I've only been able to think of one thing I want to do."

His eyes darkened, dropping to her lips, and Rose's breath stuttered.

In one swift movement, Leo drew her to her feet. His face bent over hers, and he hovered there for a moment, his eyes on her lips. When she made no move to step away from him, he pressed his lips down on hers, gathering her the rest of the way into his arms.

She sank against him, the world spinning as she was thoroughly kissed for the first time in her life. Her arms rose of their own volition, tangling in his hair and pressing his face more firmly against hers.

He responded with a sound deep in his throat, his arms tightening, and Rose's thoughts sputtered back into life.

What was she doing? She had come to Lanover with a single intention—to not fall in love with Prince Leo.

She wrenched herself away from him, breathing heavily. His eyes still look dazed, taking a moment to come back into focus. When they did, he seized her hands, speaking before her confused brain could think of anything to say.

"Posey, what are your parents' names?"

"Wh…What?" Rose stared at him, her scrambled brain struggling to keep up. Everyone in the Four Kingdoms knew the names of her parents.

Then she remembered. She was Natalie.

She withdrew her hands, placing them against her head as she tried to make sense of the tangle she had let her life become. She had just kissed Leo—the one person she had sworn not to love—and he didn't even know her true identity.

"They're…it's…Dane and Patti," she stammered, dredging the names of Natalie's parents from her memory.

"And your grandparents?" he asked eagerly.

"I…I…"

A cloud of confusion dimmed his expression as he watched her clear distress. But Natalie had never told Rose the names of her grandparents. Why would she?

And even if she'd known the names, Rose didn't want to give them. She and Leo had just kissed, and she didn't want any more falseness between them. She didn't know *what* she wanted between them, but it wasn't that.

Mumbling an apology, she fled from the room, ignoring the cries of "Posey!" that followed her out.

INTERLUDE

LEO

Leo wrenched his mind away from the feel of Posey's soft lips against his. It had been everything he had imagined and more.

But every time he thought of their kiss, his chest tightened as he remembered the way she had pulled out of his arms and run from the room when he asked the names of her grandparents. Surely she knew her own lineage.

She had to know because Leo desperately needed her to know that information. Lanover had many things that set it apart from other kingdoms, and one was the quirks in their various laws of succession. Leo didn't care about most of them, but there was one that had been occupying every moment of his waking thoughts since his kiss with Rose. Before a crown prince of Lanover could become betrothed, he had to present the name of his intended to the royal council for approval—along with the names of her parents and grandparents. It was a legal formality—the council had never refused the royal choice—but it was still a requirement.

He paced up and down the room, considering the issue. It was possible Posey didn't know her own ancestry. His parents had faced the same problem since his mother had grown up without knowing her birth family. But they had succeeded in tracking down the necessary answers. Posey didn't come from Lanover, though, so it wouldn't be nearly as easy.

He threw himself into an armchair by the fire only to leap back to his feet almost immediately. He would travel to the mountain kingdom himself if necessary. It had to be possible to find the names of her grandparents.

He resumed pacing. Why did such an archaic and ridiculous law still exist? Why hadn't his grandparents repealed it after it caused so much trouble for his father?

He ran a hand over his face. His parents had only just taken the throne. They wouldn't think it was a good time to challenge the royal council—not even for the sake of their beloved son. So it would be up to him to find the answers.

He once again felt the weight of Posey in his arms and groaned, his pace increasing.

"Slow down, Leo," said a laughing voice from just inside the door. "You're going to wear a hole in Uncle Frederic's favorite carpet. He might never leave you in charge again."

Leo spun to face his cousin, grateful for the distraction. "There you are, Luca! I've barely seen you the last few weeks."

"I've been too busy obeying orders." Luca strolled further into the room. "Orders issued by you, I might add. Some thanks I get."

Leo raised an eyebrow. "Ha! I have eyes in my head, you

know. I'm well aware those orders haven't been causing you any hardship. So don't pretend you haven't been enjoying yourself. I must say, the princess is nothing like the dutiful, well-trained royal my parents were expecting—I don't know what they were thinking." He shook his head. "She's beautiful enough, though, which is all I promised you. So you can hardly complain."

Something flashed in Luca's eyes, although he quickly turned his gaze away from Leo to hide it.

Leo frowned, his own gaze turning sharp. Had that been anger? Was Luca angry that Leo had spoken disparagingly about Princess Rose?

Fresh worry churned in his gut, adding to his worries over Posey. He had thought Luca was treating the entertainment of Princess Rose like a game, and Leo had been pleased his cousin was enjoying himself. But that quickly hidden emotion had nothing to do with lighthearted flirtation.

"You can't be serious, Luca," he said sharply, his panic rising. "Don't forget what I said at the beginning. Her parents won't let Rose leave Arcadia for anything less than a future crown. Any other man who marries her will be expected to join her there."

Luca shifted uncomfortably, his eyes sliding away from Leo, and Leo's anxiety grew.

"They expect me to run an entire kingdom one day, Luca." His words held an edge that he couldn't rein in.

Luca had been there from Leo's earliest memories—plunging into trouble at his side but taking the consequences alongside him just as stoutly. Leo's father had recently taken on the kingship, but he'd done it with his younger brother at his side as Chief Advisor. When Leo had asked how his father managed the pressure, he'd said that he didn't bear it alone. He had both his wife and his brother, Cassian, at his side.

Leo had felt relieved, knowing that he might not have a brother, but he had a cousin who was as good as one. When Leo's turn came to take the throne, he would have just as strong a team as his father did. And with Luca at his side, he would still have the link that tied him to his childhood and the carefree boy he had been in those years. Without Luca, Leo's inner self might entirely disappear beneath the weight of the crown.

Luca couldn't abandon Leo for Arcadia. He couldn't. Luca had sworn his future to Lanover, just as Leo had—first when they were children and again when they turned eighteen. Leo might be the one to wear a crown one day, but he had never thought of the burden as his alone to bear.

"We don't know that for sure," Luca said. "Lila seems to love Lanover. She might…"

Leo shook his head. "What about your suspicions? You kept insisting Rose had some sort of hidden agenda. I thought you were just getting swept up in whatever game you were playing—finding ways to make your duty more interesting. But there might be something in it. Have you tried investigating?"

Luca hesitated. "I suppose it's foolish, but I want her to tell me herself. I want her to trust me enough to share her worries with me."

Leo's face tightened. "Trust is essential. If there's no trust between you, Luca…"

"Why do you think I'm so eager to find out what it is she's holding back?"

"You're sure there is something?" Leo felt the weight of yet another worry.

"There's something there," Luca said quietly. "I'm sure of it."

Leo wanted to leap on Luca's words. To convince him that Rose was a dangerous deceiver and he should have no more to do with her. But he forced the impulse down.

"Are you sure it's not just that she was given the same instructions I was given?" A cynical note crept into Leo's voice. "She probably came here aiming to become a queen. My parents told me she's very dutiful—even if I haven't seen any sign of it myself."

Luca looked away, hiding his expression. But Leo caught enough of a glimpse to read his emotions. Luca hated the thought of Rose pursuing Leo even more than he disliked Leo criticizing her.

Leo imagined the situation in reverse. How would he feel if Posey was more interested in Luca than she was in him?

His chest tightened in a spasm so sharp it was painful, and his gut churned sickeningly. He quickly pushed the thought away. Posey had never paid Luca any attention.

But as the sensations faded, so did his earlier indignation. He had been sure he couldn't be crown prince without his cousin at his side, but that had been before he met Posey. If he faced a future without Luca's support, he wouldn't face it alone. If Posey would have him, he knew they could bear any burden together.

He still wanted to have Luca at the Lanoverian court.

He had always imagined their future wives forming their own bond—the four of them not just family but friends as his parents were with his uncle Cassian and aunt Tillie.

But feeling as he did about Posey, how could he fight to deprive Luca of that same connection? Leo couldn't see the attraction in the feisty, inconsistent princess, but if Luca truly cared about her, Leo couldn't work against them.

He intended to fight for Posey with everything he had, so he had to let Luca do the same with Princess Rose. And at least the match might soften his parents toward his own choice. They couldn't be disappointed in him if Luca achieved the Arcadian marriage alliance in his place. Luca becoming part of the Arcadian royal family would strengthen the connection between the two kingdoms almost as much as Princess Rose becoming Lanover's future queen.

"Rose isn't interested in me," he told Luca in a quiet voice. "It's utterly obvious that she doesn't look at me at all. She's too busy looking at you. I don't think we've had a single conversation that wasn't stilted."

"Stilted? Lila?" Luca laughed, his brow clearing. "She doesn't have any issue speaking her mind with me."

Leo clapped him on the shoulder. "If she does have a secret, you'll work it out. Maybe it's that she has no more desire to marry me out of duty than I have a desire to marry her."

"No, you don't want to marry her," Luca said, his usual grin returning to his eyes. "Gratitude is the most you feel."

Leo raised his brows. "Gratitude?"

Luca's lips twitched. "For bringing her friend with her to Lanare."

"I don't know what you're talking about," Leo said stiffly, even knowing his cousin would see straight through him.

It was the first time in his life he'd had something he didn't want to share with his cousin. But he'd only realized belatedly that Posey wasn't from Lanover and wouldn't have understood what it meant for him to ask the names of her parents and grandparents. She hadn't realized it was a declaration of his intentions, instead running from the room without knowing the extent of his feelings. She deserved to hear his heart before Luca did.

Luca didn't press him, though—he just laughed. "I'm not so distracted by Lila that I haven't noticed how you've been spending all your time—the time I freed up for you. But keep your secrets for now. I'm sure the whole kingdom will hear about it soon enough. And then you'll be wanting me to shield you from Uncle Frederic and Aunt Evie." He shook his head, but he was still chuckling as he left the room, his good humor fully restored.

Leo watched him go with a sigh. He hadn't predicted the consequences of asking Luca to distract Princess Rose. But he wouldn't have given up the past weeks with Posey for anything. In that short time she had not only wrapped herself around his heart, she had already helped him make Lanover a better place.

Nothing about Princess Rose had impressed him, despite his parents' assurances. Posey, however, would make an incomparable queen.

CHAPTER 14

Rose ran blindly through the palace, fleeing from the confused mess of her feelings. But they were wedged in her heart and followed her wherever she went.

She finally slowed her steps, recognizing her location by the hubbub of noise emanating from the dining hall. The evening meal must be in full swing.

How long had it been since she had bumbled her way inside for breakfast on her first morning? It felt like a lifetime ago. And there was no chance she would go unnoticed in the hall now. Far too many of the servants had seen her in the interview room with Leo—they wouldn't welcome her intrusion on their turf.

She turned to walk away, but her steps faltered. One person was waiting for her to appear in the dining hall— Aurora's agent. With everything that had been going on, Rose had forgotten all about him and the problems of Arcadia. She had become so wrapped up in Lanover's problems—and in Leo himself—that she had forgotten her duty to her own people.

How long had it been since she had even wondered about the thief and the letter that had never appeared? Too long.

She turned reluctantly back toward the dining hall, hesitating as she tried to force herself to enter. She had nothing to report to the agent, but at least she could get an update from him.

But she was still standing uncertainly at the door when an indrawn breath drew her attention. The footman in question stood a few feet away, stopped short on his way into the dining hall.

"I'm sorry," she began, but he cut her off with a quick shake of his head.

Within seconds, he had whisked her into the same storage room as the previous time. When the door shut behind them, he turned to her expectantly.

"Have you heard from the thief? When there was no word from you in all this time, we thought he must have changed his mind. Or that our information had been faulty."

"No, I never received a letter," Rose said. "I'm sorry I've been no use at all. I just came for an update."

The man watched her, a speculative gleam in his eyes. "You've been busy with other matters."

Embarrassment washed over Rose, but she straightened her shoulders. She wasn't ashamed of what she'd been doing for Lanover.

"Yes, it has been busy."

"There was some debate among the agents as to

whether you were still interested in the matter of the missing seal." He said the words carefully.

"Of course I am!" This time Rose did flush. "I've been distracted, but I still care."

"In that case, you have good timing. Approaching you has been complicated given you spend all your time with the crown prince, but there is time-sensitive information you should know."

"Something's happened?" she asked sharply. "What is it?"

"We need you to act as liaison," he said. "Most agents don't have positions of authority, and the few who do are with the tour. Even the Dowager Duchess of Sessily—who has long operated as liaison between Aurora's network and the Lanoverian crown—is with the tour. Even her son is away from the capital."

"This isn't a matter for the Lanoverian crown anyway," Rose said resolutely. "It's a matter for the Arcadian crown, and I'm their representative here."

"If you insist." Despite the man's cautious words, he looked relieved to be able to hand responsibility to Rose. "We still haven't definitively identified the thief, but we're certain he's in league with the forgers. Unfortunately, that's a problem because there are increasing signs that the forgery ring is breaking up and preparing to leave Lanare. If that happens—and if the thief goes with them—we may lose him forever."

Rose sucked in a breath. "And the stolen seal along with him."

"Not to mention any documents he's already made with

it," the footman said grimly. "He's had plenty of time to make a damaging number of false documents by now."

"We can't let them leave!" Rose cried. "You know where the building with the red door is—you need to stop them."

The agent didn't move, showing no discomfort as he spoke. "That isn't our role. We aren't in a position for that sort of overt action. Guards are needed for that. I can provide information, but you're the one who has to decide if you wish to involve guards and move against the ring."

"I need to organize a raid on the forgery ring?" Rose asked blankly.

"If you deem it to be in the best interests of your kingdom. As I said, there are some among our number who have doubted whether you would wish to make such a move."

"Of course I do! I just don't know…" Rose drew a breath. "Tell me all the information you can."

The agent nodded and proceeded to explain exactly how to identify the building in question. "I would recommend moving as quickly as possible. They may already have moved out some of their operation."

"But—" She stared at him blankly. She hadn't brought any guards with her from Arcadia, and she knew nothing about organizing a raid.

The footman bowed. "I'll leave it in your hands, then."

Before Rose could think of a suitable reply, he'd left the room. She stood there alone, mind spinning. Her fingers rose to her lips. Too much had happened that day for her to make sense of any of it.

But she needed to force her mind to work. The agent had said haste was necessary, and she could hear Natalie's disparaging voice criticizing people who dithered. Rose couldn't afford to dither.

But the fact remained that she had no guards to call on. Her parents hadn't sent any Arcadian guards to Lanover as a gesture of good faith, placing their trust in the Lanoverian guards to protect her. But that meant Rose had no one to command.

However, it also meant that Rose had been given permission to use Lanover's guards as if they were her own. If she needed guards, she would have to make use of Leo's. Her first stop needed to be the guard barracks.

She hurried out of the palace, making straight for the administrative building attached to the barracks. Inside she stopped at the first large office which contained a guard captain sitting behind an enormous pile of papers.

"I need a squad of guards," she said, still panting slightly from her haste. "Or maybe two."

The guards brows slowly rose as he examined her from head to foot. "Do you now, Miss?" Rose stiffened at his tone, but he continued. "I've got quite enough work to do without people joking around."

"I can assure you, I'm not joking," she said in her iciest voice.

The captain hesitated at the instinctive note of command in her voice, but after a second examination of her, he sighed.

"Look, I don't know how things are done in the mountains, but here the guards aren't a public resource to be commandeered at will by all and sundry. And they're certainly not to be used in personal squabbles."

Thunderstruck, Rose stared at him. The mountains?

After talking with Aurora's agent as her true self, she had completely forgotten that most of the palace still knew her as Natalie. The guard captain wasn't seeing Princess Rose of Arcadia, commandeering guards as part of a royal exchange, he was seeing a commoner girl from the mountain kingdom.

She opened her mouth to claim her true identity, but her words stalled in her throat, and she closed it again without speaking. She had been living in the palace for weeks, happily playing the role of Natalie. Why would this random guard captain believe her if she suddenly claimed to be Princess Rose? At best, he would kick her out unceremoniously. At worst, he would drag her off to Leo to let the prince deal with her delusional claims.

Holding her head high, Rose left the office without another word. It was past time to tell Leo the truth—that much was clear. But she didn't want a random guard captain in attendance for that conversation. Nor did she want it to begin with someone declaring her to have delusions of grandeur.

But when she walked back into the palace, she turned toward Natalie's room, not Leo's. Natalie had been faithfully acting in Rose's place for weeks. Even with Rose stealing all Leo's time, Natalie had still fulfilled the terms of the swap.

Rose needed to give her warning of what she was about to do. Natalie might even want to accompany her to talk to Leo. Rose couldn't deny she had the right, although she preferred to confront Leo alone.

Every step she took carried her closer to reclaiming her true name and position. Relief blossomed inside her, unfurling leaves that stretched and curled all the way through her.

She had thought she was freer without her title weighing her down, but being Natalie had been restrictive in different ways. Rose had experienced firsthand some of what had driven Natalie to want to become a queen.

Maybe everyone had aspects of their life that felt imposed and foreign to their true selves. Maybe navigating that reality was something everyone had to learn to do. Leo had said he could be a responsible crown prince and still have fun—that his old mischievous self was still a part of him, even now he was crown prince.

Rose's experiment had proved the same was true of her. Posey and Princess Rose weren't two separate people. They were two facets of the same whole, both an integral part of her. When she had tried to live just as Posey, she had constantly fallen back into Princess Rose. Trying to separate the two had been a futile effort, and one that would only cause harm if she allowed it to continue. Together she and Natalie would end their ruse.

But when Rose let herself into Natalie's room, the other girl was nowhere in sight. From the look of the room, Natalie had just finished elaborate preparations for an evening event, and all three maids bustled around, restoring the room to order. Rose tried to remember what had been scheduled for that night and failed.

"Where's Natalie?" she asked. "I need to talk to her at once."

"She's at the ball, of course," said Donna. "As she should be, considering it's the final event of the season and being held in honor of you."

Hilary shook her head. "She's as bad as the other one."

"What do you mean?" Rose asked. "Are you talking about Natalie?"

The three maids exchanged looks, and Donna sighed. "Not too long ago, she came rushing in here just like you did. And she was saying she needed to urgently talk to you as well."

Rose's eyes widened. "She did? I need to find her immediately."

"She's at the ball!" Hilary sounded scandalized. "You can't rush into the ballroom looking like that."

Rose looked down at herself, frowning. She looked respectable enough, but it was true that she'd become somewhat bedraggled over the course of the day. And she certainly wasn't dressed for a royal ball.

"That isn't what's important—" she began, but Cate cut her off, apparently too frustrated to worry about insignificant matters like status.

"Of course it's important! Eventually everyone is going to know you're the true Arcadian princess, and you can't turn up to your own ball looking like that! It won't take us long to get you ready, and if the two of you are so desperate to talk to each other, then it's fortunate you'll both be at the ball and can do as much talking as you like."

"Something you won't be able to do if the footmen refuse you entry," Donna added warningly.

Rose deflated. "Fine, then. But be as quick as you can. It doesn't matter what I look like. I just need to look fancy enough that they won't stop me at the door."

Even as she said the words, a traitorous part of her thought of Leo. He would surely be at the ball.

But it didn't matter whether he thought she looked more beautiful than the other girls. He had kissed her while she was dressed exactly as she was.

She put her hands to her suddenly burning cheeks, and the maids exchanged another round of looks, Cate bursting into giggles.

"No need to wonder who you're thinking about," she said archly, making Rose snatch her hands from her cheeks.

"I'll run and fetch a gown from your room," Hilary said briskly. "Donna, you start on her hair."

Hilary hurried from the room, and Rose forced herself to sit down at the dressing table and hold still while Donna's quick fingers worked on her hair. It seemed a long time but was likely only a few minutes before Hilary arrived back, out of breath. Joanne was only steps behind, reverently carrying a dress Rose had yet to wear. Her parents had ordered it especially for the trip, but she hadn't attended many formal evening events.

Rose couldn't help a slight lift to her heart at the sight of the filmy peach material. She had loved the dress during her fittings.

The maids helped her into it, and Joanne sighed with satisfaction when they stood back to regard the result of their efforts.

"Now you're looking like a princess," she said. "As you should. It's past time for this nonsense to end."

"You're quite right," said Rose. "I've let it go on far too long. That's why I need to talk to Natalie."

The maids exchanged surprised and pleased looks, but there was something else there as well. A hint of guilt?

Donna stepped forward. "We should probably confess that we may have been a little untruthful with Natalie tonight. She was just as heedless of the ball as you, but one of you had to turn up! We told her you'd instructed us to make sure she attended and to make sure she did so looking like a princess." She frowned in judgment. "Both of you have been so busy lately that no one has been considering your duties."

Rose winced. Given the way she had lambasted Natalie on the beach, Natalie had no doubt believed the maids' words without question. Rose would have to apologize to her at some point. It was Rose's fault if her duties had been ignored, not Natalie's.

She sighed. "Well, now we're both going, so I hope all four of you are satisfied." She relented and gave them a small smile. "I do appreciate you keeping quiet all this time."

"As long as you're truly returning to your proper place now, that's all we want," Cate said.

"It will happen tonight," Rose promised.

CHAPTER 15

Rose arrived at the ball unheralded, but at least the footmen outside didn't bar her entry. She stood for a moment at the top of the stairs, using her vantage point to scan for Natalie.

But the footman behind her cleared his throat warningly, and she was forced to descend into the ball. The crowd—full of constant movement and laughing voices— made it hard to locate anyone. If only she had Leo's height.

As if on cue, he appeared at her elbow. The admiration in his eyes made her momentarily forget everything else, and for a second, she was back in the interview room, his arms holding her close, his lips against hers. She flushed.

"Dance with me." The soft words were less a demand than a certainty. Leo clearly knew how irresistible she found him—and given the speed with which he had appeared at her side, perhaps he felt the same.

She let him take her hand, lost again in the confusing swirl of emotions she had felt after their kiss. From the beginning of her time in Lanover, and despite all her intentions to avoid him, she and Leo had found their way to each other over and over again. Even while pretending to be Natalie, they had been drawn to each other.

But he still believed her to be someone she wasn't. She had let him kiss her under false pretenses, and he deserved the truth. Would it change the way he felt about her? It might—given the way he had avoided the girl he believed to be Princess Rose.

And what of herself? Was she willing to embrace the strength of her feelings, even if it meant meekly doing what everyone demanded—and leaving her home and family in the process? As the future queen of Lanover she might occasionally make brief visits to Arcadia, but she would never live there again. Could she accept that?

Leo pulled her into the dance, and the feel of his strong arms answered the question in her mind. In Arcadia she wasn't even needed as the spare anymore—not when Harry and Charlotte would be starting their own family. But in Lanover she had already made a difference. In Lanover, she could share a future with Leo.

But Leo hadn't actually proposed—or even spoken of love—despite their kiss and the look in his eyes when they rested on her. Instead he had asked about her family. He clearly cared about her background, and she shouldn't make the mistake of assuming an increased rank would mean a better position in his eyes. He might still feel as she had felt on arrival—that the one person in all the kingdoms he wouldn't marry was Princess Rose of Arcadia.

He was smiling down at her, but a small, concerned crease lingered between his eyes. She wanted to forget the watching audience and reach up to smooth it away. She wanted to tell him that she'd been foolish and made too many mistakes, but that despite herself—against her wishes even—she hadn't been able to help falling in love with him. She wanted to tell him her heart and ask him to help her kingdom.

She should have trusted him and asked for his help from the beginning.

She couldn't wait any longer. Hopefully Natalie would understand. Rose would beg Leo not to tell anyone else until she had warned Natalie. He would be willing to wait —as long as he wasn't furious with her over the deception. But either way, Rose couldn't keep waiting.

She smiled up at him, her feelings in her eyes, and opened her mouth to speak.

But he spoke before she could, his voice strained.

"There's something I have to do." Abruptly he released her, taking a hasty step backward and nearly colliding with another pair of dancers.

She staggered slightly at the sudden loss of his support, her eyes flying back to his. But his face was set in deter-mined lines, and he wasn't looking at her anymore.

"Leo," she began, conscious they were causing an obstruction on the dance floor. But he was already striding away, weaving through the dancers.

A whirling couple nearly collided with Rose, and she muttered an apology, hurrying off the dance floor as directly as possible. Once she was out of the dancers' way, she would find Leo and demand to know what was wrong —because clearly something was wrong.

The song wound to a close as she reached the edge of the ballroom, and she struggled to find him in the mass of moving people. When she finally caught sight of his head above the crowd, she moved toward him. But she hadn't made it far before she realized he wasn't alone. He stood extremely close to Natalie, his hand on her elbow.

As Rose watched, astonished, he led Natalie into the next dance.

Her mind went blank. He had left her and gone to Natalie. Of course he had. *Princess Rose* was the one he was supposed to marry, not Posey. He had probably been toying with Posey all along, always intending to pursue the supposed princess.

She had narrowly escaped telling him the truth when his feelings had never been real. She didn't want a husband who only married her because of her rank—even if that husband was Leo.

But even as her mind screamed the defiant thoughts, she knew she was being silly—overreacting to the insignificant hurt of being abandoned on the dance floor in favor of Natalie. She didn't really believe Leo was insincere and false. She wouldn't have given him her heart if he was that sort of person.

He had behaved strangely, but there must be a reason for it. She needed to find out that reason, not react with knee-jerk anger like a small child.

She circled the dancers, trying to keep the two of them in her sight. Leo spun Natalie to the edge of the dance floor and deftly maneuvered them both out of the dance. Rose picked up her pace as Leo led Natalie outside into the garden. The nearest section of greenery had been lit with decorative lanterns, and he took her just far enough that they were alone while staying within the light cast by the lanterns.

Rose slipped out behind them, the only one willing to brave the stern expression Leo was using to warn everyone else away. She stopped once she was close enough to hear their words, arriving just in time to hear Leo speak.

"I realize I should have spoken to you sooner." He sounded stiff and formal, nothing like the way he talked to Rose. "I'm aware that our parents had certain hopes for this visit, and that you may have come here with certain expectations yourself. I shouldn't have waited so long to clarify my position, and I hope I haven't caused any pain on your end. While I value Lanover's alliance with Arcadia, I have no intentions of pursuing a marriage alliance with you now or ever."

Rose stumbled back a step, her heart contracting and her stomach churning as she heard him say the very words she had been fearing only minutes before. He had decided against her before he ever saw her, just as she had done with him. Would he still hold to that opinion when he found out the truth?

Natalie opened her mouth to respond, but something stopped her. Her gaze swept their surroundings and fastened on Rose. Her eyes lit up, her face begging Rose to step in. But Rose's feet had grown roots and her tongue was dry in her mouth.

Leo cleared his throat, clearly uncomfortable and worried about offending Arcadia. "I mean no slight on your personal charm, of course. I know my cousin—" he cut himself off. "What I mean to say, is that it's not about you personally at all. I know that as crown prince, my duty is to my kingdom, and I intend to dedicate my life to Lanover. But I cannot love where I am instructed to do so. I refuse to even attempt it. Love shouldn't be about cold-blooded gain."

But what if your heart couldn't help it? Rose wanted to wail the words. To beg him to reconsider. If love was warm and true, shouldn't they celebrate the incidental gains that happened to come with it?

Natalie looked at her again, clearly trying to communicate something without words, but Rose's gaze was too focused on Leo to absorb the other girl's expression.

"Please stop, Prince Leo." Natalie held up a hand as a barrier between them, stepping back to give herself space.

"I truly mean no offense." He sounded worried again.

"None is taken," Natalie said swiftly. "At least by me. However, you might feel some offense when you hear the truth. So please bear in mind that I also meant no offense. Neither of us did."

Rose jolted as she finally realized what was happening. Natalie was telling Leo what was Rose's responsibility to tell. She should have stepped in like Natalie's eyes had asked her to do. She still should.

But her feet still refused to move, her tongue still stuck to the roof of her mouth.

"Us?" Leo sounded oddly relieved. "Are you talking of Luca?"

"Luca?" Natalie stared at him. "No. Why would I be—?" She shook her head. "I'm talking about Princess Rose and me."

He frowned. "I don't understand. You are Princess Rose."

"Actually, I'm not. I'm Natalie. And she's me. I mean—" Natalie's words grew hopelessly tangled. "I mean that the girl you know as Natalie is the real Princess Rose."

"Posey is Princess Rose?"

Rose could read nothing of Leo's feelings in his voice and face. Both were devoid of all expression, leaving the ground beneath her feet uncertain. Was he horrified? Disgusted?

"Posey?" Natalie must not have heard the nickname Rose had chosen.

"That's what Natalie said she preferred to be called…I mean…Rose said?" He paused before continuing. "You're serious?" His face and voice still gave nothing away. "The companion who arrived in Lanover with you is the true Princess Rose?"

"Yes, Your Highness. I'm very sorry for deceiving you. We only intended to do it for a few days as a…game of sorts, and meaning no disrespect to you or the Lanoverian court. But then—"

Natalie's gaze found Rose, another plea in her eyes. But Leo turned his head to follow her gaze, finally seeing Rose.

Their eyes met and suddenly Rose could move again. She needed space—she needed to make sense of the overwhelming emotions flowing through her. She took off into the gardens.

Behind her, footsteps pounded on the gravel in pursuit.

CHAPTER 16

"*P*osey, wait!" A pause. "Rose!"

Her proper name brought her up short, stopping her heedless flight. The steps behind her slowed as well, Leo approaching more carefully now that she'd stopped running.

"Is it true?" he demanded of her back. "Are you really Princess Rose?"

She turned slowly, drawing a deep breath as she moved. It was time to stop guessing and wondering about his feelings. She needed to ask him directly and accept whatever answer he gave. She could do no less after misleading him for so long.

"Yes, it's true," she said softly.

"And you did it as a game?" He sounded hurt.

She bit her lip, wanting to give the most honest answer she could.

"Not really. That was just…an excuse. I did it because I wanted to be free."

"Free? Of me?" His words came quickly, his eyes intent on hers.

She forced herself to continue with the honesty. "Yes, in part. But also not really. It was never about you, of course. I didn't even know you then. It was what you represented."

His brows drew together. "And what did I represent to you, Princess Rose of Arcadia?"

"Duty. Obligation. A future I didn't get to choose. I've always been a dutiful princess, but I was starting to feel like I couldn't breathe. I wanted to know what it felt like not to be Princess Rose. I thought accepting your courtship meant accepting that I would never be more than my title." She gave a wry smile. "Not that you made any effort to court Princess Rose, as it turned out."

He broke into sudden laughter, throwing his head back and laughing helplessly. When his mirth finally subsided, he shook his head. "Apparently you heard what I said back there. I was just as determined as you not to initiate any courtship. I even commissioned my cousin to help me. And look how that's turned out." He took a step closer, but Rose took one back, and he stopped, letting her maintain the distance between them. "How did it feel? Not being Princess Rose?"

Rose briefly closed her eyes, wincing. "It turns out there's no escaping Princess Rose. She's just as much me as Posey is." She peeped up at him. "As you might have noticed."

His lips twitched. "It does make sense of a number of things. That was definitely Princess Rose in the interview room with me for all those interviews."

Rose groaned. "Yes. I've done a particularly poor job of acting my part recently. I couldn't help myself, it turns out."

"If you can't help being yourself, that's a good thing."

"But I lied to you," she said. "And I'm so sorry for it. It was a foolish waste of time and effort, too. Since it turns out I was totally incapable of not falling in love with you."

Light sprang into Leo's eyes. He took another step forward, and this time she didn't retreat. He closed the distance between them and took both her hands.

"Do you really mean it? You love me?"

She swallowed. "How could I not? You're charming, kind, intelligent, entertaining—and you truly care about people." A flush crept up her cheeks. "And you must be aware of how you look."

He tried to suppress a smile and failed. "How unfortunate that my parents turned out to be right. They'll never let me forget it."

"Your parents?"

He nodded. "They told me that Princess Rose was perfectly suited for me and would make an excellent queen one day. I stubbornly refused to believe it, thinking they were only seeing what they wanted to see. But it turns out they were correct on both counts."

Rose sucked in a breath.

"And I don't think it was wasted time and effort at all," he continued. "While I hope you'll never have reason to deceive me again, I understand why you did it. Of all people, I can understand wanting to be free of a suffocating role—I spent a childhood fighting it with Luca. It took me years to understand how to combine all the parts of me. If it only took you weeks, you're doing better than I did." His eyes smiled down at her, and she smiled back.

He pulled her closer, his mouth resting against the top of her head. "I'm even glad you did it," he murmured. "Otherwise, I might have stubbornly kept avoiding you. How can I be angry about a stratagem that gave me a chance to get to know you?"

Rose buried her face in his chest, wrapping her arms around his waist. "If you put it like that, I'm glad I did it too. The two of us would have been determined to get in our own way."

He squeezed her, and for a minute she lingered there, resting against him and reveling in the peace and joy of the moment. But all too soon, he leaned back, giving enough space for her to look up at him.

"When I asked the names of your parents and grandparents, I forgot that you wouldn't know what that meant."

"It did seem a bit odd," she admitted. "But I shouldn't have run out. I didn't know the names of Natalie's family, and I didn't want to give them to you anyway—I didn't want to lie to you when we'd just kissed—so I panicked." She leaned back further, putting more room between them, although he kept his arms loosely around her. "Why did you ask?"

"In Lanover, there's a legal technicality that has to occur before the crown prince can become officially betrothed. I have to present the name of my intended, along with the names of her parents and grandparents, to the royal council for approval."

Rose stared up at him. "You mean you were saying that you..."

He smiled tenderly down at her. "Yes. I got a bit swept up in the moment, so it wasn't the most romantic proposal. But all I could think about was presenting you to the council and getting approval. I didn't need to know your title to know you would make a brilliant queen. So, Princess Rose of Arcadia, will you marry me?"

Rose took a slow breath, feeling the weight of her future. A thrill ran all the way to her toes, but she couldn't resist teasing him a little.

"Are you sure they'll approve me, though? I wouldn't want to get my hopes up only to be disappointed."

Leo shook her lightly, laughing. "Of course they'll approve you. They'll be jumping over themselves to say yes. I predict they already have a draft treaty and will whip it out the moment I make the request." His voice turned stern, although his eyes still smiled at her. "But what I'm interested in is your answer. What do you say, Posey? Will you share my future and help me bear the crown one day?"

"Of course I will," she said. "But not out of duty. I'll marry you because I chose you—and you chose me."

Leo's head dipped down, his lips pressing gently against hers, a wealth of promise in the gesture. They would have a lifetime for future kisses.

Rose was the one to pull back, her brows pulling together. "I'm willing to commit my future to Lanover—I already love your kingdom. But before I do so officially, I need to do one last thing for Arcadia. And I need your help to do it."

"Of course," he said immediately. "Whatever it is, you have my help."

She grinned. "Shouldn't you find out what it is first?"

He laughed. "I trust you, Rose."

She breathed in the words, letting them steady her. "I had to tell you the truth first, and I couldn't help getting distracted by…this." She gestured between them. "But according to Aurora's agents, we need to move quickly." She filled him in on everything she knew about the situation.

He gave an exasperated groan. "You should have come to me about this at the beginning! Or asked Natalie to speak to me on your behalf, I suppose. Aurora told us about the theft weeks ago."

"What?" Rose's eyes widened. "She told Lanover our secrets?"

"Don't be offended," he said quickly. "She doesn't tell us everything. But she knew what you apparently didn't—that we could be trusted to want to help Arcadia with this."

Rose sighed. "Let's not lose any more time, at least. Can you gather guards right now? I can lead the way to the building."

"There's no need for you to come," Leo said quickly. "I don't want you in any danger."

Rose shook her head stubbornly. "If you want me to marry you, you have to let me do this last thing for Arcadia."

Leo sighed. "Then we both go. Right now. I want to announce you as my bride as soon as possible."

CHAPTER 17

Rose stood outside the red door, Leo at her side. Two squads of guards had spread out to encircle the building.

"All entries secure, Your Highness," the captain said. "Are you intending to enter yourself?" He looked deeply disapproving of the idea.

Leo looked at Rose.

"I'm going in," she said firmly. "Those are highly sensitive Arcadian documents we're hoping to find. I should be the one to retrieve them."

Leo pressed his lips together but didn't argue. "We're both going in," he told the captain. "There hasn't been a sound from inside, so there aren't likely to be many people in there—if any. Pick five of your best guards to accompany us."

The captain saluted and barked orders to his men. Five of them joined the royals, four with swords in their hands. The fifth held a drawn bow.

Leo nodded, and the first of the men put his shoulder against the door, bursting it open and stumbling inside, two of his companions rushing in behind him. One of them was the archer.

Only silence greeted them.

Rose hurried forward in their wake, not waiting for the others. They could bring up the rear.

Inside, evidence of a hasty departure littered the space. Chairs had been overturned, and papers lay scattered across tables and the floor. She stooped to retrieve one and scanned it before letting it float back down. It had nothing to do with Arcadia.

The most important thing to retrieve was the seal, but she wanted Arcadia's documents—and any false ones the thief had created—almost as much. She hurried forward, ignoring the guards as she moved through a series of rooms. Clearly the building was already empty. They had come too late.

Most of the papers she checked appeared to be drafts— obvious errors making them unusable as forgeries. The fleeing forgers must have taken both the stolen samples and the clean copies with them.

She ground her teeth in frustration, increasing her pace, despite the warning call from one of the guards. A half-full cup of tea sat abandoned on a table, and she brushed her fingers against it. Residual warmth still remained. Had they missed their targets by only minutes?

Her feet slowed as her brain worked on the problem. The forgers had clearly fled in haste and recently—as if in response to the arrival of the guards. But if that was the case, they should have been spotted fleeing. Leo's guards had approached the building from all directions.

She stepped into the last room. It was the largest she had yet seen, with a substantial fireplace and eight desks. And one occupant.

Rose froze in shock, staring across at the woman who was busy stuffing papers into a satchel slung over one of her shoulders. The woman looked up, meeting Rose's eyes and freezing herself. But she launched back into movement more quickly than Rose.

Seizing the last of the papers, she was already turning away as she stuffed them into her bag. But she didn't move toward Rose and the only doorway. Instead, she pressed her hand against the bookshelf behind her.

Her body blocked Rose from seeing exactly how it was done, but the fireplace creaked in response to the woman's actions, swinging open. A secret passageway! That's how they'd escaped.

Rose sprang to life and threw herself across the room after the woman, shouting for the others as she ran. There was no time to wait for them, though. The bookshelf was already swinging closed.

She lunged the final distance and wedged her fingers into the remaining gap, wincing as the bookshelf tried to close on her hand. Straining, she pulled it back open and hooked her leg around the closest desk, dragging it close enough to wedge the bookshelf open.

Answering shouts and footfalls sounded from the guards, converging on her from other rooms, but she still couldn't wait for them. She had no idea where the tunnel exited—if she waited too long, the woman would escape out the other end and be lost forever.

Rose threw herself into the dark opening, almost tripping down the short flight of stairs behind the bookcase.

"Posey!" Leo's voice sounded from behind her.

Rose didn't slow, but she did feel a stab of relief to know he was so close behind her.

The darkness made it hard to run at full speed, but she moved as quickly as possible, hands held out in front of her. When her fingers ran into a dirt wall, she groped around until she discovered the tunnel turned leftward. Thank goodness it hadn't been an intersection. She would have had no idea which way to turn.

Following the tunnel, she increased her pace as the darkness slowly lightened, allowing her straining eyes to see the faintest outline of the tunnel walls.

The light grew, growing stronger and stronger until she stumbled out into another room. On this side, nothing blocked the tunnel opening, and there were no stairs.

She appeared to be in an unfinished basement, although she could see no clue as to what sort of building lay above them. She didn't care either. All her attention was focused on the woman. She had turned to look at Rose in alarm, apparently not realizing Rose had made it into the tunnel.

Rose straightened her dress, wishing she wasn't wearing a ball gown. "I believe the papers in your bag belong to me." She held out a hand. "I suggest you give them back immediately. I'll tell the guards following me that you cooperated."

The woman snarled. Before Rose realized what she was

intending, she leaped forward and seized Rose, dragging her back away from the tunnel opening just as Leo burst out of it.

He froze, his eyes widening at the sight in front of him. The woman held a knife against Rose's side, her other arm holding Rose firmly in place.

Rose met Leo's eyes, trying to send a silent apology. She should have been more cautious.

"Let me leave, and I'll let the princess go," the woman said.

Rose gasped. If the woman recognized her, then she'd probably been with the thief in Arcadia. Perhaps she even was the thief, although Aurora's people had been sure it was a man.

"You have our seal," she cried angrily. "Give it back at once."

The woman pressed the tip of her knife against Rose's side with enough force to pierce the bodice of her dress. "I'm the one making demands."

"I suggest you unhand Princess Rose at once," Leo said in the coldest voice Rose had ever heard from him.

His eyes flashed dangerously, and she shivered. The woman behind her held firm, however.

"Let me go, and I'll release her unharmed out on the street."

"There's no way I'm letting you leave here with her." Leo clenched his fists, every muscle taut.

The woman began to slowly maneuver Rose to the right, toward the main basement door, keeping Rose between her and Leo. Rose went without resisting, but her eyes darted around the space, looking for anything that might let her break free.

Nothing stood between them and the door except a large, solid wood table. It would have to do.

As the woman edged them past one of the table's corners, Rose held her breath, waiting for the right moment. Just as she was about to pass out of reach, she latched her fingers around the edge of the table and held on with everything she had.

The unexpected anchor took her captor by surprise, and Rose jerked out of her hold. The sudden loss of resistance sent Rose sprawling sideways, away from the woman and the door.

Leo didn't hesitate. Springing forward, he leaped on the woman. Rose screamed his name, twisting to see what was happening. The forger no longer had a hostage, but she still held a knife.

But when Leo arose from the scuffle, he had the woman firmly in hand, both arms twisted behind her back. The knife lay on the ground, and he kicked it away from them.

Rose gasped, sinking back to clutch the table for support.

"Are you all right?" she asked breathlessly. "Are you hurt anywhere?" Her eyes ran over him, looking for injuries.

"I'm fine." He gave her a quick smile before resuming his stern glare at the woman.

Rose took a long breath, her heart rate finally slowing. Now that the immediate danger was past, her thoughts returned to what had driven her in the first place.

"Where's her bag?" she asked. "She seems to have lost it

in the—" She broke off and darted forward, retrieving the satchel from where it had fallen to the ground.

Guards poured out of the tunnel, exclaiming in surprise at the sight of Leo's prisoner. Two of them took the woman from him, holding her firmly from both sides, and Leo gave a quick series of orders. Three guards escorted the woman back into the tunnel, one of them carrying a lantern. The other guards disappeared into the building above them, gone to look for anyone else who had escaped through the tunnel.

Leo took Rose's hand and pulled her toward the tunnel. She followed him willingly, eager to stay close enough behind the guards to catch the edge of their lantern light.

With a lantern to light the way, the walk back felt short, and they soon popped out into the large room with the desks. The guard captain met them there. Leo conveyed the situation in a few words, and the man was soon barking orders to the rest of his men, several of whom hurried back into the tunnel with fresh lanterns.

Rose didn't watch them go, however. Drawing to one side of the room, she stood by the fireplace and examined the contents of the bag. The last of the tension drained out of her.

Every one of the missing Arcadian documents was inside, along with several piles of false documents. The only disappointment was that there was no seal hiding at the bottom.

She stared down at them for a short moment, and then flung them away from her into the fire that still burned in the fireplace. One floated in the wrong direction, and she retrieved it, shoving it after the others. Picking up a poker, she stabbed at them, making sure they went deep into the flames.

"You've burned them?" Leo asked in surprise from behind her.

She nodded, her eyes still on the flames. "It's not that Arcadia needs them—it's that they're dangerous in other hands. Especially in company with the stolen seal."

She remained in place, determined to stay there until she had personally seen every last piece of paper turn to ash.

"The seal?" Leo asked, and she shook her head.

He put an arm around her waist, holding her from behind. "We'll find it. We have a prisoner now, and she can tell us the identity of the rest of the forgers and hopefully the seal too."

Rose sighed. "If it's not already gone from Lanover."

"Ahem." An uncomfortable throat clearing made them both turn to the poor guard who hovered awkwardly nearby.

"Yes?" Leo asked, not removing his arm from Rose's waist.

"I've just arrived from the palace, Your Highness. I was sent with a message from Prince Luca."

That got Leo's attention, and he released Rose to turn and face the man fully. "Luca sent you out here with a message for me? What is it? Quickly now!"

The man cleared his throat. "He was demanding to see you, and when he heard where you'd gone, he thought you'd want to know his information right away. He and the princess—" The guard hesitated, his brow creasing as he looked at Rose. "Ah, he and the other princess arrested a man in the palace. He was one of the palace gardeners, and he attacked the…ah, other princess, and tried to kill her."

"He tried to kill Natalie!" Rose gasped and stepped forward. "But who is he? What does he have to do with this?"

"Prince Luca said to tell you that officially the gardener is to be tried for attempted murder, but that, unofficially, he's also a thief. His Highness said to tell you that he's retrieved the *item of greatest significance.*"

The guard looked curiously between them, clearly hoping for an explanation. But Leo dismissed him with his thanks, and the man was forced to leave.

Rose swayed, relief robbing her of balance. Leo caught her, pulling her safely against him.

"What excellent fortune," she murmured. "They've found the seal for us and even arrested the thief. But I can't believe Natalie was attacked! I hope she wasn't hurt." She tried to take it all in. "I guess Aurora's agent was right. The thief did have a position at the palace."

"Another thing we can blame our old steward for," Leo said grimly. "He brought in so many unsavory characters that one more was easily able to slip through the gaps."

Rose shivered, and he held her tighter.

"Don't worry," he murmured. "Luca wouldn't let anything happen to Natalie. And if she *was* hurt, he wouldn't be sending me messages. He wouldn't be thinking of me at all."

Rose pulled away, startled. "You don't mean…?"

Leo chuckled and nodded. "That's exactly what I mean. Your ruse brought more than one couple together. And now, about that. I've helped Arcadia as you requested, and even endured seeing you held at knife point. Please tell me I'm allowed to claim you publicly as my fiancée now?"

Rose blushed. "You can tell anyone you like because I don't intend to let go of you, Leo of Lanover."

He smiled, pressing a quick kiss to her lips, despite the guards still moving about them. "I'm utterly relieved to hear it."

"I'm sorry you have to wait because of me," Rose said to Natalie, looking at the other girl's reflection. The two girls stood side by side in front of the enormous full-length mirror that stood in Rose's new and equally enormous royal suite.

As Leo had predicted, the council couldn't give their approval fast enough, and her new suite had only been one indication of their pleasure at Leo's choice. Rose had appreciated the gesture since it allowed Natalie to keep the room she had been using since her arrival. But as she looked at their reflections, she felt a stab of guilt. Only one of them was wearing a wedding gown.

Natalie looked stunning in one of the purple dresses being worn by Rose's attendants, but Rose knew how much her friend was looking forward to her own wedding. If it had been up to Leo and Rose, they would have happily had a double wedding with Luca and Natalie, but being crown prince came with certain expectations. King Frederic had insisted that Leo be married first and with all possible pomp, so Natalie and Luca had been forced to wait.

"Don't be sorry," Natalie told her. "You have to squeeze every drop of happiness out of today! I don't mind waiting. Luca and I will get our turn soon enough."

"Goodness," said a new voice, in tones of astonishment. "Whatever have you done to Natalie? I think you've wrought a miracle."

Rose laughed as she turned to greet her sister-in-law. "It wasn't me. Unless you count agreeing to swap places with her. The rest she did herself."

"I'd heard rumors," Charlotte said gravely. "Mostly from Natalie herself. But I didn't entirely believe them." She laughed. "Not the swapping places bit—that I believed easily." She raised her eyebrows. "Although I was a little surprised to hear you'd agreed, Rose."

Rose tried to look guilty and failed. She was too happy at the outcome to regret her foolish prank.

"Good on you," Charlotte whispered as she drew close, one hand resting protectively on the slight bulge of her belly. "It always worried me that you were so consumed by your role. You were so helpful to me when I first arrived in Arcadia, teaching me how to be a princess. I appreciated it enormously, but I felt sad that it was the only life you'd ever gotten to know."

Rose smiled. "I've come to terms with that now. Being a princess is too much a part of me for me to separate myself from it. I don't even want to now." She snuck another glance at herself in the mirror. Soon she would be Leo's wife.

"I'm very sorry you're staying here permanently,

"They're going to meet us outside the throne room," Natalie said.

"Are you nervous?" Charlotte asked, squeezing Rose's arm.

"What does she have to be nervous about?" Natalie asked. "At least she won't be expected to do laundry in that stunning gown." She wrinkled her nose while Charlotte laughed.

Rose looked at Charlotte with wide eyes. "Is it true, then? Is that really a required part of wedding ceremonies in the mountain kingdom? I thought Natalie was teasing me."

"I'm afraid to say it is," Charlotte said. "Although I heard Gwen means to change that."

"She's always been a sensible sort," Natalie said approvingly.

"Unlike you," Charlotte laughed.

Natalie looked wounded. "What do you mean? I've always been very sensible."

Charlotte kept laughing. "Like when you assured me you were going to become a queen."

Natalie joined her laughter. "Maybe not, then. But you have to admit I was very helpful during the rebellion. I had some excellent ideas."

Charlotte grinned. "I acknowledge it freely. And I'm sorry you were cut out afterward. Gwen told me about that."

Natalie sighed. "I've done my best to let that go. I still don't agree with what my parents did, but I think I understand it better now. Things aren't always as black and white as I used to think. Sometimes there's no easy answer."

"So you aren't holding on to any regret about not becoming a queen?" Charlotte asked. "If it was anyone else, I'd say you were uncommonly fortunate to manage marrying a prince at all, but you have always pulled off feats no one else could achieve."

Natalie shuddered dramatically. "No regret whatsoever. I'm relieved I failed at that goal. If I learned anything in our swap, it's that I would make a terrible queen. Rose will do an infinitely better job, and Luca and I can support her and Leo from the side lines. That will suit me much better."

She hesitated, glancing at Charlotte before she continued. "I've even talked to Luca about searching for Baden."

Charlotte's eyebrows rose at the mention of Natalie's brother. But Natalie had already talked it through with Rose, and she approved.

"That would be a big step," Charlotte said cautiously. "I know you always had strong feelings about him."

Natalie shrugged. "I still do. But I can see his situation in a different light now. He might have betrayed us, but he was two years younger than I am now at the time, and he was scared and wanted to protect his family. I think I'd like to hear his side of things." She sighed. "It's not as if I always make the right choices myself."

Charlotte smiled. "I hope you do manage to find him. I heard no one's had any news of him since his banishment."

"Luca said he'll help me search." Natalie laughed. "I think he's actually excited about the prospect—a legitimate reason to go off adventuring."

"The challenge will be stopping Leo from joining him," Rose said ruefully.

"We'd love to have you," Natalie immediately declared. "Didn't Leo say he intends to be both responsible and adventurous as crown prince?"

Rose laughed. "Something like that."

"As long as you stop in Arcadia on your way to your adventure then I heartily approve," Charlotte said. "But for now, there's a different sort of adventure waiting for you, Rose. Are you ready for it?"

"Utterly and completely ready," Rose said with her biggest smile. "There's no adventure I want more than to spend a lifetime at Leo's side."

If you've enjoyed my Four Kingdoms fairy tales, consider trying my new fairy tale world, Kingdoms of Legacy—starting with Legacy of Roses: A Beauty and the Beast Tale.

Or if you missed first meeting Natalie as she helps stage a rebellion, read the two books in the Four Kingdoms duology now available in a single volume, To Ride the Wind and Steal the Sun.

To be informed of my new releases, as well as new bonus shorts, please sign up to my mailing list at www. melaniecellier.com. At my website, you'll also find an array of free extra content in my Four Kingdoms world.

Thank you for taking the time to read my book. I hope you enjoyed it. If you did, please spread the word! You could start by leaving a review on Amazon or Goodreads or Facebook or any other social media site. Your review would be very much appreciated and would make a big difference!

ACKNOWLEDGMENTS

I hope you've enjoyed this second part of my retelling of The Prince and the Pauper. Originally, I was determined not to write stories for any of the children of the original Four Kingdoms characters, but I'm so glad that both Alyssa and Max's kids have now gotten their own story.

I enjoyed writing about Rose, and I hope you enjoyed reading her perspective, even if she didn't get a full-length novel. I'm so grateful to my whole team who helped to bring her story to life.

To Lyra, Karri, Mary, my parents, Rachel, Priya, James, Rebecca, and Esther—thank you once again for helping me bring together every aspect of my story and book for publication.

And, as always, thank you to God who stays with us through all generations.

ABOUT THE AUTHOR

Melanie Cellier grew up on a staple diet of books, books and more books. And although she got older, she never stopped loving children's and young adult novels.

She always wanted to write one herself, but it took three careers and three different continents before she actually managed it.

She now feels incredibly fortunate to spend her time writing from her home in Adelaide, Australia where she keeps an eye out for koalas in her backyard. Her staple diet hasn't changed much, although she's added choc mint Rooibos tea and Chicken Crimpies to the list.

She writes young adult fantasy including books in her *Spoken Mage* world, her *Mage's Influence* world, and her various *Four Kingdoms* and *Kingdoms of Legacy* series that are made up of linked stand-alone stories that retell classic fairy tales.